# JAKE MARCIONETTE
# JUST JAKE

illustrated by
VICTOR RIVAS VILLA!

Grosset & Dunlap
An Imprint of Penguin Group (USA) LLC

I DEDICATE THIS BOOK TO MY MOM & DAD! THANKS FOR ALL YOUR LOVE AND
SUPPORT, YOU TWO ARE THE BEST! . . . AND TO MY LATE GRANDMA AGNES
FOR ALWAYS TELLING ME "WHAT TO DO IS UP TO YOU!" . . .
THANKS, GRANDMA, I MISS YOU!

ACKNOWLEDGMENTS: THANK YOU TO MY SISTER, ALEXIS, FOR GIVING ME SO
MUCH MATERIAL TO WORK WITH BY JUST BEING YOU!

GROSSET + DUNLAP
Published by the Penguin Group
Penguin Group (USA) LLC, 375 Hudson Street, New York, New York 10014, USA

USA | Canada | UK | Ireland | Australia | New Zealand | India | South Africa | China

penguin.com
A Penguin Random House Company

ISN'T IT COOL THAT
SPEECH IS FREE?

Text copyright © 2014 by Jake Marcionette. Illustrations copyright © 2014 by Victor Rivas Villa.
Published by Grosset + Dunlap, a division of Penguin Young Readers Group, 345 Hudson Street, New York, New York 10014.
GROSSET + DUNLAP is a trademark of Penguin Group (USA) LLC. Manufactured in China.

Library of Congress Cataloging-in-Publication Data is available.

ISBN 978-0-448-46692-7                                    10 9 8 7 6 5 4 3 2 1

# TABLE OF CONTENTS

ALEXIS DID THIS!
LAME.

# CHAPTER 1
# WAKE UP!

← CHEAP!

The hotel's cheap alarm clock blared inches away from my head. I jumped out of bed in an absolute panic. It sounded like the room had been invaded by an eighties metal band.

Bug-eyed and frantic, I saw my dad standing in the bathroom doorway already dressed and ready to go.

"Nothing like a little Guns N' Roses to get the adrenaline pumping," he shouted over the deafening radio.

"Come on, Dad! It's 5:00 a.m. You said we could sleep until seven. Are you kidding with that alarm?" I protested.

"Sorry, Jake," he said. "A good soldier has to adapt to

any and all circumstances. We need to bug out a bit earlier due to road construction. It's a long trip to Maryland, so we need to get a move on."

Mom and Alexis still hadn't moved a muscle, even though the alarm was screaming away. It takes a special ability to be able to sleep through anything. Evidently, I didn't inherit my mom's comatose gene.

Dad hauled the first load of luggage off to the car and instructed me to wake the two Sleeping Beauties. "Well, now that I'm up . . . with pleasure!"

I decided to tackle the most difficult assignment first. My big sister, Alexis, routinely treated me as her personal punching bag. To make matters worse, she HATED being woken up. This amounted to a lose-lose proposition for me. But I wasn't going to let my dad down. I hoped Alexis would be too sleepy to go completely ballistic.

YOU NEED A FEW TRANQUILIZER DARTS BEFORE APPROACHING ALEXIS!

I approached my sleeping teen sister as cautiously as a game warden would an anesthetized lioness. They know they need to get that radio collar on the animal, but they're terrified the beast is going to wake up.

———————————————————————————

I considered the situation for a second. Maybe I could just start whacking her with my pillow till she gets up. No, no, no . . . an early-morning hospital visit would be MOST unappreciated by my dad and I needed to make it to the car in one piece.

Realizing what I had to do, I went in.

"Alleeeexxxxxxiiiiiisssssssss," I cooed in my most soothing "baby" voice. Braced for the worst, I jumped back, anticipating a violent explosion of arms, pillows, and blankets.

NOTHING!

I tried the angelic approach one more time, but again, no sign of life. Dad wasn't going to appreciate my lack of effort. He had given me a task, and I intended to complete it. The third time had to be the charm, and I had a plan.

Approaching Alexis in pure stealth mode, my target was her beloved teddy bear, Mr. Chuckles. Very carefully, I rescued the bear from a nine-hour headlock. It was time for Chuckie to enjoy an unscheduled makeover.

I started wrapping the bear in toilet paper. I was going for a mummified look—very ancient Egypt. Mr. Chuckles looked a little parched, so I grabbed Alexis's water bottle and splashed his face with some refreshing $H_2O$. Mr. Chuckles was finally ready for his face-to-face with Alexis.

Shoving the furry little King Tut into Alexis's face for a BIG WET MORNING KISS probably wasn't my proudest moment. But my dad had ordered me to wake up Sleeping Beauty, so a soggy kiss from Prince Chuckles was the perfect solution! I knew Alexis would finally wake from her slumber. And she did!

As she opened her eyes and furrowed her brow, the shriek in her voice assured me I had scared her good. "Mr. CHUCKLES!?!?!" she wailed, followed by a slight pause and a refocused priority. "YOU!! You are DEAD!"

She grabbed me by the shirt collar, and it took everything I had to break free. However, we were in a crowded hotel room with two double beds, and I didn't have much room for evasive maneuvers. Alexis was immediately on her feet and in pursuit of her tormentor.

My only chance was to make it to the bathroom. Backing into the TV stand, I turned to run for the safety of the flimsy door and its push-button interior lock. Unfortunately, I didn't see the load of luggage my dad had placed neatly in front of the closet door.

BOOM! Down I went. Still thinking I had a shot to make it to the bathroom, I started crawling like an infant on his first playdate. My arms and legs were moving surprisingly fast, and I seemed to be cruising along . . . or so I thought. Actually, I wasn't moving at all.

DON'T TOY WITH ME, BRO!

Quickly, the excitement of my "escape" gave way to the downward pressure of a giant foot placed on the small of my back. Alexis wore a size 9½! She had caught her prey and was toying with me like a cat with a mouse.

Flipping me over onto my back, Alexis pinned my face to the ground. Knowing about my severe germaphobia, I'm sure she enjoyed smashing my cheek into the sticky floor. I immediately envisioned a swarm of bedbugs infesting my hair. GROSS!!

The struggle was escalating and getting louder by the second. Seriously, Mom, how do you sleep through this?!

"Torturing Mr. Chuckles isn't very FUNNY. He has FEELINGS!" Alexis said with an extra thrust. "Is the hotel floor tasty?"

Then, like the bugle call of the cavalry coming to the rescue of a surrounded wagon train, I heard the unmistakable sound of a plastic room key being inserted, followed by the glorious *click* of the automatic door release. I looked up to see my dad's smiling face.

"Great work, Jake! I didn't think you'd ever get her up. Way to go! Where's Mom?" Dad asked, as he stepped over us to collect luggage load number two.

With all the bags packed, checkout complete, and everyone accounted for, we were finally leaving Florida. It's funny how life is sometimes like baseball, with the pitcher suddenly throwing you a massive curveball you didn't see coming. One moment you're the King of School, the next you are dethroned and in search of a new kingdom in Maryland.

Piling into the car, we were all exhausted. Except for the Big Guy! He was into his second cup of coffee and barking orders. I pretended to be too sleepy to understand. Acting like a morning zombie, I grabbed my favorite pillow and backpack and headed to Slumber Town. Wake me when we get to the amazing I-95 roadside attraction, South of the Border! As "Pedro" says, Jake needs more fireworks!

Dad was not buying my sleepy act. He expected everyone to check, double-check, and CHECK AGAIN.

THIS IS NOT PEE.

"Keys?" CHECK.

"Directions?" CHECK.

"Everyone go to the bathroom?" OOPS! I appreciated the reminder.

Dad HATES last-minute inconveniences. He shot me a look of utter amazement.

"ARE YOU KIDDING ME!" Dad bellowed as I climbed out of the car and headed back into the hotel. I kept quiet, figuring it was best not to say anything. No need for a lecture on proper planning and time management. It's WAAAAYY too early for that.

That's Dad's specialty: telling someone what they did wrong and how they can improve. He actually does it for a living. He's a management consultant, and companies basically pay him to analyze (aka *harsh on*) their businesses and tell them how they need to improve (i.e., how much they SUCK!).

I don't know why anyone would pay to be yelled at, but I guess I can't complain. I get three square meals a day. Wait a minute!! I CAN complain . . . because of his stupid job, I had to leave the Sunshine State for MARY-land. What the heck is Maryland the state of, anyway? I know the University of Maryland mascot is a terrapin. So I'm giving up white-sand beaches, beautiful blue skies, Disney, and fantastic citrus for the state of slow-moving turtles? Fantastic!

WE'RE HEADED DOWN DA OCEAN, HON!

MAN, HE'S SLOW.

# CHAPTER 2
# AWESOMENESS

If you've ever tried sleeping in the backseat of a car, then you know how tough it is to get quality *zzzs*. Especially when your incredibly selfish sister keeps stealing your pillow.

Since she outweighed me by a few TONS, I decided to let her have it. No need to get the honey badger all riled up so early in the trip.

I NEED MY ZZZS!!

Yes, Alexis was big and mean, but at the end of the day, she was no match for me. Why? Because, unlike my dear sister, I was born with an extraordinary talent that's superior to brute strength: AWESOMENESS! It's a gift that keeps giving every day and takes many forms.

See, with a name like Jake Ali Mathews, I had a lot of pressure on me from the start. My dad gave me the middle name Ali after Muhammad Ali, who is considered the best boxer of all time. His nickname is "the Greatest." Thanks, Dad! No pressure here!?!

Growing up, I got teased a ton about my name and my size.

I wasn't exactly the biggest kid on the playground. So I learned early on how to improve my chances for survival by developing my crazy ability to know exactly what adults want to hear, one of the many benefits of AWESOMENESS. Some might think of me as a scammer or a suck-up, but that's just because they're not me.

I also understand the social hierarchy of middle school,

like I understand sports. I know how the game is played and how to ALWAYS end up on top. Add to the equation my incredible intuition—sometimes it feels like I can predict the future—and a pit bull-like work ethic, and you have yourself AWESOMENESS in a nutshell.

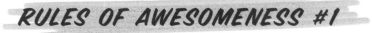

## RULES OF AWESOMENESS #1

LOOK OUT FOR *NUMERO UNO*—THAT'S YOU!
I CAN ONLY PLEASE ONE PERSON PER DAY . . .
AND THAT PERSON IS ME.
FOR EVERYONE ELSE, SORRY, BUT TODAY IS NOT YOUR DAY.
AND TOMORROW IS NOT LOOKING GOOD FOR YOU, EITHER.
DON'T STRESS, THOUGH, BECAUSE YOU, TOO, CAN FOCUS
ON YOU. GET IT? PUTTING "YOU" ABOVE ALL OTHERS DOES
SOUND A TEENSY-WEENSY BIT SELFISH, BUT
YOU'LL GET USED TO IT.

Come to think of it, pit bulls probably don't worry about being that AWESOME. I'm sure they're very happy just terrorizing mailmen, appearing in music videos, and wearing cool spiky collars.

Not everyone appreciates this character trait. Some of

my classmates accuse me of taking myself too seriously. But middle school is serious business. I work hard to put myself in a position to crank the winning goal in lacrosse. Or go to the state science-fair finals. If I'm not pushing the limits of AWESOMENESS, then I'm not doing my job. Don't hate the player, hate the game!

Truth be told, my AWESOMENESS gets me into trouble from time to time, but the benefits are well worth the occasional black eye. My favorite use for my inexplicable AWESOMENESS is when I wield its mighty power against my HATERS.

And there is no bigger HATER than my diabolical sister, the Queen of Mean! She keeps me on my toes and is a worthy adversary. But even Alexis, with her fake tears and ability to lie and not crack under parental interrogation, is no match for Jake the AWESOME.

For example, not so long ago, I decided to turn on the TV while enjoying my breakfast on the couch. Alexis doesn't get to watch TV in the morning, so I knew she would be angry when she saw me enjoying my ESPN. In my house, only honor-roll students enjoy that luxury. I think Mom is really onto something there.

Knowing exactly what she would do, I strategically concealed my cell phone in the bookcase to record über-aggressive Alexis attacking me to regain control of the TV remote.

Like a great white following one of those cutout seals the Shark Week guys tow behind their boats, Alexis soon came tearing into the living room to pounce. Too easy!

In my attempts to capture the elusive Alexis in her natural environment, I always remember to take precautions. Plenty of pillows and cushions surrounded me as I awaited impact. A guy can get really hurt messing with a perfect killing machine.

You need to understand, Alexis is no ordinary eighth-grade girl. She looks like a typical dorky drama llama with long blond hair that she takes great pride in for some reason.

She's preppy and can be polite, especially when our parents are around. Alexis is no dummy! She knows Mom and Dad hold the keys to her future—and the keys to a new car once she turns sixteen. Alexis plays the parent game well, but looks are deceiving. She's freakishly strong, superathletic, lightning fast, and MEAN.

Put it this way: She's the only girl I've ever seen join a boys' lacrosse team. Alexis had no fear of strapping on the pads and helmet and bodychecking boys twice her size. She absolutely dominates.

And, of course, she HATES me like a good sister should, and my AWESOMENESS drives her crazy. If I were her,

I'd hate me, too. I'm always two steps ahead of her feeble attempts to get me.

That morning at breakfast was just another example of how AWESOMENESS defeats AGGRESSION every time. After the attack, and a quick presentation of video evidence to Mom, Alexis was banished to her room for an hour of folding laundry. I slid back into relaxation mode with my favorite show and a second bowl of cereal. CHOMP! CHOMP!

Note to Alexis: I like my socks together, tightly rolled up in a neat little ball.

## RULES OF AWESOMENESS #2

WORRYING ABOUT THINGS YOU CAN'T CONTROL IS A COMPLETE WASTE OF TIME AND ENERGY.
KIDS HAVE A LOT GOING ON THESE DAYS, SO WORRYING ABOUT SOMEONE OR SOMETHING NOT WITHIN YOUR CONTROL IS FOOLISH AND POTENTIALLY SELF-DESTRUCTIVE. LET'S TAKE ALEXIS, FOR EXAMPLE. SHE CAN NO MORE DESTROY MY AWESOMENESS THAN SHE CAN STOP THE SUN FROM SETTING OR THE MOON FROM RISING. JUST LIKE HOW I KNOW HER CLEATS WILL ALWAYS SMELL LIKE SKUNK ROADKILL AND THAT SHE WILL NEVER ACCEPT MY FRIEND REQUEST ON FACEBOOK.

No doubt the Chuckles makeover infuriated Alexis and ignited her quest for revenge. Sitting within arm's length of me in a cramped backseat for a nine-hour car ride provided Alexis with the perfect chance to deliver payback. But was I worried? Not one bit! I had AWESOMENESS on my side.

As soon as Alexis awoke from her sleep-a-thon, I saw that look in her eye. She was bored, angry at being uncomfortable, and looking for trouble. Time for action!

"DAD! Can you please remind Alexis about backseat-boundary rules," I implored.

Mom was asleep in the front, so I knew Dad would jump at this opportunity to set guidelines that would guarantee a hassle-free drive.

"Hello, sweetie, nice to see you awake," Dad said sarcastically to Alexis, shaking his head and giving me a look of assurance in the rearview mirror.

"Yes, Jake is absolutely correct. In order for you two knuckleheads not to fight the entire trip, remember, your side of the seat starts at the door and ends at the armrest. DO NOT cross into Jake Territory. If you do, severe and swift penalties will be handed out. Namely, your cell phone WILL be confiscated and held until the end of the journey. DO YOU COPY?"

Alexis didn't know what hit her. One minute she was blissfully sleeping, and the next she was facing the ULTIMATE penalty in our house—cell-phone repo!

## RULES OF AWESOMENESS #3

THE BEST DEFENSE IS A GREAT OFFENSE.
NEVER SIT BACK AND BE THE VICTIM. ALWAYS BE ON THE OFFENSIVE, AND WHEN NECESSARY, SEEK THE AID OF A LARGER, MORE POWERFUL ALLY. PARENTS AND TEACHERS WORK PARTICULARLY WELL IN THIS ROLE.

Once again, game . . . set . . . MATCH. There is nothing my dad hates more than backseat rumbling when he is trying to read his maps.

That's right, no turn-by-turn GPS in our car. Dad still relies on these crazy giant folded sheets of paper to get us

from point A to point B. And the slightest distraction, especially during the refolding process, causes him to become unhinged.

Going straight to cell-phone repo was a bold move, but not unexpected. I knew that would keep Alexis contained and quiet for the rest of the trip . . . and keep me BRUISE-FREE!

# CHAPTER 3
## KID CARDS

Alexis went back to doing what she does best—SLEEPING, with a little bit of drooling.

As I stared out the window, I noticed the landscape quickly change from palm trees to pine. I tried to stay positive. *How exciting!* This was going to be great. Just then, I noticed my Kid Cards shoe box on the floor of the car.

I smiled to myself, proud of my craftsmanship. "What are Kid Cards?" you ask. Only the coolest thing ever! Think baseball cards, but the team is your school and the players are your classmates. I've been a doodler for a while. When I was a youngster, I drew lots of silly stuff, like monsters and spaceships.

But, as I got older, I switched it up
and started sketching just people.

Way back when, in Mrs. Bucket's incredibly
boring class, I took it to the next level with
goofy stick figures of all the kids in my grade.

I'M NOT SO BAD!

Then I added some
action and funny captions to
keep it interesting. Soon, each kid had his or
her own page in my notebook.

I'M BORED!

When the notebook got too
packed and bulky, I needed to shrink
everything down in order to better
manage my creations. Also, these beauties are
for MY EYES ONLY. I don't want to share them
with anyone. So, reducing each drawing to the size
of a playing card made sense.

But I didn't stop there. I dropped
the stick figures and tried to draw
the actual kid. Unfortunately for the
"larger" kids, I'm not the world's best artist.
Skinny kids I can draw well. But normal to larger
kids end up looking more egg-shaped, like Humpty
Dumpty. I'm still working on my technique. Sorry,
Frankie . . . at least you
won't crack!

Lucky for me, my mom had an old
lamination machine at home. Strange,
right? Yeah, I know, but when I was
younger, Mom was an arts-and-crafts
queen! We had an entire room filled with beads,
ribbons, glue sticks, and fabric.

I remember making tons of cool stuff with Alexis—
back when she was fun and didn't care about Facebook
updates, friends, and the mall! Mom always played classical
music, or she'd put on a CD of a bunch of people speaking

Chinese. That was weird. As if we could understand what they were saying. Mom said it didn't matter. It was important to "experience another language."

We'd sit for hours doing projects, painting, and playing with Legos. Looking back, we were basically guinea pigs in Mom's experiment to create supergeniuses. Once again, I can't complain. Schoolwork, by comparison, is easy. Try being locked in a room all day listening to Mandarin while painting landscapes. THAT'S difficult.

So I dug out the old laminator, and before long, all the cards looked like they were professionally made.

I kept my new creations in a small box for safekeeping. I couldn't risk showing them to other kids because . . . let's just say many of the cards weren't exactly flattering.

But I did take great pride in the cards' professional appearance, as each was meticulously created, following a strict Kid Card template. Being responsible for each kid's historical footprint, I needed to be objective and

thoughtful in my assessment. Yes, like everything else in life,
I took this project SERIOUSLY!

Here is the template I followed for each Kid Card:

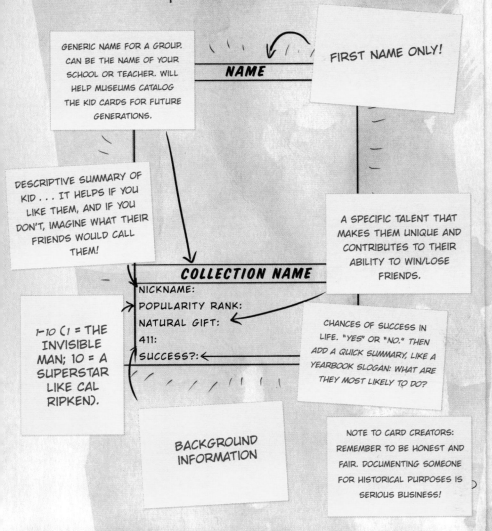

GENERIC NAME FOR A GROUP. CAN BE THE NAME OF YOUR SCHOOL OR TEACHER. WILL HELP MUSEUMS CATALOG THE KID CARDS FOR FUTURE GENERATIONS.

FIRST NAME ONLY!

**NAME**

DESCRIPTIVE SUMMARY OF KID . . . IT HELPS IF YOU LIKE THEM, AND IF YOU DON'T, IMAGINE WHAT THEIR FRIENDS WOULD CALL THEM!

A SPECIFIC TALENT THAT MAKES THEM UNIQUE AND CONTRIBUTES TO THEIR ABILITY TO WIN/LOSE FRIENDS.

**COLLECTION NAME**

NICKNAME:
POPULARITY RANK:
NATURAL GIFT:
411:
SUCCESS?:

1-10 (1 = THE INVISIBLE MAN; 10 = A SUPERSTAR LIKE CAL RIPKEN).

CHANCES OF SUCCESS IN LIFE. "YES" OR "NO." THEN ADD A QUICK SUMMARY, LIKE A YEARBOOK SLOGAN: WHAT ARE THEY MOST LIKELY TO DO?

BACKGROUND INFORMATION

NOTE TO CARD CREATORS: REMEMBER TO BE HONEST AND FAIR. DOCUMENTING SOMEONE FOR HISTORICAL PURPOSES IS SERIOUS BUSINESS!

Kid Card example:

**LOUIS**

**SUPERHERO SCHOOL**

NICKNAME: FLY KID
POPULARITY RANK: 9.5
NATURAL GIFT: LEAPING OVER BUSES
411: FATHER IS A FAILED SUPERHERO. ANGRY.
SUCCESS?: YES! WILL RESTORE FAMILY NAME!

**JAKE**

**KID CARD CREATOR!**

NICKNAME: BOY AWESOME
POPULARITY RANK: 10+ (FL), 3+ (MD)
NATURAL GIFT: SHARING HIS GREATNESS
411: ONE OF THE FINEST EXAMPLES OF A BOY!
SUCCESS?: IF HE CAN MAKE IT THROUGH
SIXTH GRADE

My first card,

in honor of me!

# CHAPTER 4
# BYE-BYE, FLORIDA

Opening the Kid Cards box, I gazed down upon my greatest creation—the Oceanview Collection. It consisted of cards of all my Florida classmates, neatly arranged and looking shiny and new. Why did I have to leave? Everything was so perfect.

But there was nothing I could do. That's what it's like being a kid. You go where you're told. As my dad says, "When you pay the electric bill, you get to decide where things get plugged in."

Okay, Dad, I get it, you're the boss! Hope you like commuting in the snow and ice. And that means no more beach for you either, Big Guy.

The worst part about the move was how quickly it happened. Seriously, my dad dropped the bad-news bomb about two weeks ago. The next thing I know I'm crammed into the backseat of a Nissan with Alexis the Terrible, staring at a box full of handcrafted memories.

I didn't get much time to prepare my school for the big good-bye. I knew there would be lots of tears. Who wouldn't be upset over losing their school's most prized pupil? I was like a national treasure.

I figured they would at least put the flag at half-staff . . . I know I'm still very much alive, BUT my departure meant that AWESOMENESS was leaving the building. Poor kids.

The morning after I found out, I walked into my homeroom and made a beeline for Mrs. Bunch.

"Good morning, Mrs. Bunch. I have some awful news," I said, trying to look upset.

"What is it, Jake?" said Mrs. Bunch, showing great

concern, as I knew she would.

"My dad got a new job in Maryland. We're moving at the end of the month. I can't believe it," I said, tossing in a few sniffs and heavy sighs for effect.

Mrs. Bunch froze in disbelief, like a statue you see in front of a museum. Her mouth was wide-open. *Holy cavities, looks like Mrs. B. loved the candies and soda back in the day.*

I hope I don't have to call 911. She took it much harder than I expected.

Awkward silence . . . blank stare . . . MORE silence . . . I slipped back to my desk, allowing Mrs. Bunch more time to process life without me.

Was I actually more beloved around school than I thought?! And Mom said I needed to "dial it down a bit" with all my self-confidence. What did she know? Ha! I wonder how many teachers she mummified. Next victim, please . . .

Lunch was the perfect opportunity to rip off the Band-Aid: I'll tell everyone at once so the whole school can suffer and experience their collective loss together. There is strength in numbers. I saw a giant group hug in my future.

JAKE, UNLESS YOU'RE A HAMBURGER, I DON'T THINK HE CARES.

Going table by table, I explained my situation—the move to Maryland—and said my good-byes.

Not everyone took the news the same. Some kids openly showed signs of sorrow. The bravest, toughest kids offered words of encouragement.

**LUKE**

OCEANVIEW COLLECTION

NICKNAME: PROFESSIONAL BOY
POPULARITY RANK: 3
NATURAL GIFT: BEING EXTRA ANNOYING!
411: ALWAYS LOOKING TO SUE CLASSMATES
SUCCESS?: YES! ALREADY WORKS FOR DAD

"I'm going to miss you, Jake," said Luke Ridley as he firmly shook my hand and patted me on the back. "But cheer up. Living in Maryland puts you closer to Washington, DC, and cool things like the Supreme Court and Congress!"

Many, though, held in their tears and masked their true feelings with laughter.

Molly thought she fooled me when she clapped and

**MOLLY**

**OCEANVIEW COLLECTION**

NICKNAME: WOWIE GIRL
POPULARITY RANK: 10
NATURAL GIFT: BEING BEAUTIFUL
411: GOOD-LOOKING AND AS SWEET AS CANDY!
SUCCESS?: YES! PRETTY PEOPLE SUCCEED!

let out a loud
"HOORAY!"

I don't think,
so, Molly. I know it
hurts.

By the end of that
day, my news had
the school rocketing
up and down an
emotional roller

coaster. There wasn't any relief from the pain until Mrs.
Bunch announced that Friday was "Jake's day." In just
a few short periods, my people rallied together to honor
me with a full day of outdoor classes, football, and party
munchies. I knew I was going to miss Oceanview! I was
going to miss it VERY MUCH!

Unfortunately for my family—and everyone in
town—Alexis didn't take the move as well as I did.

Probably because her teachers and classmates DIDN'T plan a day for her! I could tell she was jealous!

Her overdramatic reaction to the move was typical Alexis. Lots of tears, girlfriends sobbing, TONS of hugging, and Facebook tributes.

Every hour, like clockwork, they went into fits of "I'm going to miss you so much!" Then, cry, cry, cry . . . hug it out! Next hour: "I'm never going to have a best friend like you!" Cry, cry, cry . . . hug it out. Next hour: "Remember when

we [fill in any stupid story about the mall, the beach, bike riding, etc.]?" Cry, cry, cry . . . hug it out!

---

Her friend Mogul—YES! That is her REAL name—offered to adopt Alexis to keep her in Florida forever. I LOVED that plan! But sadly, Mom vetoed Alexis's adoption.

Even my parents were losing their patience with the dork circus and their cries of protest. On our last day of school, the dorksters made a huge poster and placed it in front of school. The HILARIOUS thing about the sign was that after reading it, I wondered if Alexis's "friends" really even liked her that much:

 **ALEXIS, YOU'RE A MEANIE, BUT I'M GOING TO MISS YOU!—SANDRA**

**ALEXIS! I NEVER MET ANYONE AS FUNNY AND ANGRY AS YOU! DON'T FORGET ABOUT ME!—LIZ**

### *ALEXIS, YOU ARE SO SWEET AND SOUR . . . YOU'RE ONE OF A KIND!*
### *—HILLARY*

Am I the only one who thinks that's funny? Translation: Alexis, you're not very nice, and good riddance!

I've been making my case to Mom and Dad about her for years. Now, I had PROOF! When no one was looking, I grabbed the sign, folded it up, and stashed it in my "Jake" box. You never know when that will come in handy.

My final weeks in Florida went by like a blur. So many good-byes and e-mails were exchanged. Even with the excitement of the move, I tried to enjoy my last days in the Sunshine State.

I really LOVED Florida. I loved the sun, finding shark teeth on the beach, big gators, Disney, and moss in the trees. With everything going on, I felt anxiety building inside me, like when you drop a Mentos into a bottle of soda.

I was able to hold it together and maintain my "no worries" exterior. But, inside, I was WAY scared! Scared to go to a new school, scared to live in a new neighborhood, and ultraterrified at the thought of having to make new friends.

**JOEY**

**OCEANVIEW COLLECTION**

NICKNAME: HAIR DUDE
POPULARITY RANK: 10
NATURAL GIFT: GREAT HAIR
411: GIRLS LOVE THIS KID. IT'S HIS HAIR!
SUCCESS?: YES! PEOPLE LIKE HAIR.

**MORGAN**

**OCEANVIEW COLLECTION**

NICKNAME: FASHION KID
POPULARITY RANK: 5
NATURAL GIFT: BEING AHEAD OF THE TRENDS
411: ALWAYS WEARS THE LATEST FASHIONS
SUCCESS?: YES! REALLY, REALLY FOCUSED

# CHAPTER 5
# RUDE MARYLAND KIDS

We finally arrived in Maryland. I was excited but WAY tired. Captain Dad told me to unpack boxes in the basement and stay out of his way. No problem. The basement is dark, and thanks to the movers, it now had my favorite couch. It looked like naptime for me!

Unfortunately, Alexis was well-rested and amped up. Smacking me in the head moments after I got comfy, she demanded I go outside with her to explore the neighborhood

"Get up, loser," Alexis snarled. "Time to scope out

da hood." Alexis was rocking a large gold chain from our Christmas-decoration box, and she had her hat on sideways, gangster-style.

"Are you sure that's the first impression you want to make?" I asked.

"We're from Florida, gotta represent!" Alexis shouted in my face.

"Easy does it, Lil Wayne. Represent what?" I asked.

"I don't know, just trying to reinvent myself here in Maryland. I can be anyone I want to be now," Alexis said, trying to act all tough.

"Reinvent yourself? Why? After working SO hard to perfect AWFULNESS, that would be a shame," I said.

The punch to my arm hurt A LOT. But, fortunately for her—and my family's—rep, Alexis dropped the chain and hat combo, and we were soon rounding the side of the house, headed to the street.

Before I made it to the front yard, Alexis grabbed me by the shirt and yanked me to the ground. With a serious look, she told me to be quiet. She pointed across the street to a large group of kids sitting on our neighbor's lawn.

They were all just sitting there, intently watching our house—and our movers. But it was no welcoming party. *Must be an exciting neighborhood! Nothing like watching guys go up and down a ramp all day.*

**HATE IT!**

With each item the movers pulled from the truck, the group let out a loud boo or cheer in response to our family's valuables. I felt like we were auditioning for some sort of reality-TV show.

— — — — — — — — — — — —

And they weren't exactly a shy bunch of kids. As a new piece of furniture came off the truck, our new neighbors would first huddle up to reach a group decision. Once the verdict was decided, they'd openly display their collective disdain or appreciation.

— — — — — — — — — — — —

When our movers pulled out the lacrosse net, everyone

cheered. But Dad's pinball
machine received many
thumbs down and
a few "What the
heck?"s followed
by the loudest
BOO yet.

   I stayed motionless in the grass, like a young springbok
hiding from a pack of ravenous hyenas. THAT'S RIGHT . . .
I said *springbok*. I love Animal Planet AWESOMENESS!

   Alexis wasn't so intimidated. As a matter of fact, I
sensed her blood starting to boil. Before I could stop Ms.
Volcanic Anger, she bolted across the lawn looking to make
a lasting first impression.

   The unfortunate local hoodlums didn't
realize what was about to hit them. A category 5
hurricane of hurt and pain was about to strike. Oh
well, back to Florida.

Not wanting Alexis to face the mob alone, I jumped up to offer some brotherly support. Staying a good few yards behind, I watched Alexis walk up to the biggest kid and get STRAIGHT UP IN HIS GRILL!

---

"Hey, nerd! Why are you stalking our stuff?!" Alexis snapped. It got real quiet, real quick.

Suddenly, a much smaller girl appeared from behind the others.

"You better not speak to my brother Jason like that!" said the girl.

*Oh no . . . Alexis snacks on girls bigger than this.*

"What?! Snooki wants a beat-down, too!" Alexis roared. Her internal crosshairs shifted to fix on the quickly retreating girl.

Just then, I had a flashback to Alexis's good-bye sign in Florida and how all her friends noted her meanness. True THAT!

Stepping between an advancing Alexis and his visibly

terrified little sister, Jason carefully held up his hands. "Calm down, calm down, newbie. We're just checking out your gear. Slow your roll!" he pleaded, wide-eyed.

"Slow my WHAT?! You need to check yourself before I WRECK yourself. How dare you disrespect me and *my* family! Is this how people in MARYLAND treat their new neighbors?" hissed Alexis.

"No, no, no . . . we were just having fun. No big deal," explained Jason.

Alexis inched closer and closer to Jason's face. He was easily five or six inches taller than her. But remember, she fears nothing. Having been in this situation myself MANY times before, I knew exactly what was coming. I call it the cobra strike.

Just when her opponent is feeling most threatened, Alexis will quickly glance away, unclench her fists and act ALL surprised. I have to admit, she is a pretty good actress.

She sometimes throws in a gasp or a very predictable

"O-M-G," but this is all done to distract her victim. If everything goes according to her plan, Jason will also look away to see what the heck she is staring at. And that will be his BIGGEST mistake.

Once he's distracted, Alexis will strike with either: (a) a lightning-quick punch to the stomach, or (b) a flying headlock—her favorite. Either of these will be followed by a double-shoulder-grab-fling to the ground.

But before Alexis could go into full rumble mode, the increasingly tense confrontation was defused by my mom's angelic voice.

"Pumpkin Pie! Jelly Bean! Where are you guys?" shouted Mom.

MOM!! Those are "inside" names . . . as in INSIDE the house ONLY! They are never to be uttered in the light of day. Is she TRYING to ruin our lives?

Alexis tried to ignore the voice, but soon my mom saw all the kids and us standing across the street. Of course, she started smiling and waving like she'd just won a game show.

Alexis knew better than to start any trouble in front of Mom.

"Looks like it's your lucky day," Alexis muttered under her breath as she smiled and returned home.

Grabbing me by the shirt, she led me back across the lawn to where Mom was waiting—still smiling and waving to the new kids. Unbelievable . . . Sometimes, Mom is clueless. As we walked into the house, new neighbor Jason shouted, "See you later, Pumpkin Pie!"

The damage was done. THANKS, MOM!!

# CHAPTER 6
# FIRST DAY OF SCHOOL

The day finally came. The first day at my new school! Can you say NERVOUS? I sure could.

OOHHHH! BTW . . . I forget to tell you. It turns out, in my GREAT new town, sixth graders don't get to go to middle school like normal kids. They do things a little different here.

Sixth graders are still in elementary school!! I thought my mom was kidding when she told me. I already graduated from glorified camp. I DID NOT want to go back to glue sticks, angry hall monitors, and double-spaced book reports. I was already a MIDDLE-SCHOOL MAN! It's

like I was being held back and had to repeat a grade . . .
NOT that I would EVER know what that was like.

Since it was the middle of the school year, I was sure
everyone had already found their best friends. And, OF
COURSE, the unofficial lunch-table seating assignments
had been chiseled in stone.

But not to worry, I wasn't going to be that dorky kid
who shows up, all new and stuff, and walks up to a table
and says, "Ah, excuse me, do you mind if I sit here?"

NEVER! That would never be me. No matter how much
my "mommy" wanted me to be THAT KID.

"Jake, you just go right into that lunchroom and
introduce yourself. Have confidence. You'll be great!" said
my mom—a MILLION times.

No way. I'm not that kid. Don't worry; I had plenty of
confidence and TONS of AWESOMENESS! But there were
certain things I just wouldn't do. Why? Because I knew
how the story would end. If I've seen it once, I've seen it
a THOUSAND times. The new dork always picks the table

with the most-popular kids—who happen to be the meanest. His polite request is ALWAYS met with a "No! Are you joking?! Of course you can't sit here! That seat and EVERY OTHER seat is taken." Right out of the gate, new dork suffers HUGE, humiliating, EPIC fail.

While I was strategizing, Mom yelled from upstairs, "Get in the car, Jake, we're going to be late!"

No more time to plan; it was time to man up. I tightened the straps on my big-boy backpack and prepared to face my fears.

I dove into the backseat of the car, and off we went. Mom was rambling on about how Queen Meanie Alexis had gone skipping into middle school an hour before. Of course, Alexis was happy to go to a new school . . . new VICTIMS!

"I'm so happy for her," I replied sarcastically. My mom looked at me through her rearview mirror and frowned.

"Be nice," she warned. "You catch more bees with honey than hot sauce."

THIS WAY, GUYS!

My mom is the champ at mixing up metaphors. Normally, I'd enjoy correcting her, but right then, I was too nervous. Sweat rolled down my back, and my knees were actually knocking together.

Arriving in the drop-off circle at school, I felt like I was walking onstage at the MTV Movie Awards. It was GO TIME. Styling my best COOL-guy strut, I took my first giant step into the unknown.

WHAT . . . THE . . .? Had I just landed on another planet? The first thing I saw was a group of kids, BOYS specifically, and ALL of them were proudly wearing SKINNY JEANS?! Oookay?

DON'T TRY AT HOME

OUCH!!

Only because I have a fashion-conscious sister was I already familiar with these so-called "jeans." They're more like sprayed-on denim. Who knew how they got those suckers on? But, more importantly, WHY!!?? Why were a bunch of dudes wearing those ridiculous pants?

Where are all the khakis, pastels, or crisp white oxfords I used to see in sunny Florida? Sure, the occasional skater dude would rock baggy board shorts and a flowing white T, but those clinging skintight jeans were CRAZY!

I don't know about you, but for me, I'm a comfort-fit clothes type of guy. Big RLX sweatpants and a Marmot pullover do the job nicely. MAYBE a pair of baggy jeans once in a while—but not TOO baggy.

When it comes to school wardrobe, the ability to remove clothing quickly is critical. In case of a fire, I want to know I can shed the unnecessary gear, stop, drop, and roll. This rule immediately eliminates tight-fitting jeans, all types of sweaters, and, of course, ASCOTS.

As you can imagine, I didn't see myself hanging out

with those skinny-jean-wearing emo wannabes. HOWEVER, guess who's first up in my new Kid Card collection?

"From Kinney Elementary, it gives me great pleasure to introduce . . . Skinny Kinney Kid!"

NO ASCOT!

As I moved swiftly past that bunch of freaks, I finally saw someone with potential. He looked confident, carried himself with a fair amount of swagger, and was certainly not a follower.

But I wasn't sure about the head-to-toe camouflage outfit. Scary! I thought I missed Halloween.

   Note to self: Always pick Camouflage Kid for hide-and-seek—he'll be impossible to find!

# CHAPTER 7
# THE NEW KID

Throwing open the front doors to Kinney Elementary,
I OOZED confidence. It was going to be a cakewalk.
Drumroll, please . . . Heeeeerree's Jake!

Mom had told me to go DIRECTLY to the front office.
*Easy enough,* I thought. Zigzagging through a sea of
kids, I made it to a room filled with confusion and utter
chaos. Everyone was running around, panic-faced teachers
were clutching stacks of books, and loads of parents were
shouting questions to anyone who would listen. Not so
easy after all. Suddenly, I was flooded with fear and
anxiety. *Who's in charge here?*

Stepping toward the front desk, I sheepishly asked for Mrs. Leaf, just like my mom had instructed. The guy with the phone to his ear barely acknowledged my presence. He looked at me sharply, turned, and walked off without saying a word. Wow, welcome to RUDE ELEMENTARY! I was glad my mom hadn't walked me in. However, at that point, I could have used her help.

Mrs. Leaf suddenly appeared. Again, no *Welcome* or *Nice to meet you, young man.* Just a quick *Hi, Jake,* and a slip of paper thrust into my hand. It simply said:

NEW STUDENT: Jake Mathews

TEACHER: Mrs. Williams

She guided me out into the fast-moving flow of arriving students and pointed down the hall to the left. With a slight nudge, I was off to find Mrs. Williams's class.

— — — — — —

Kind of like a mouse in a maze, searching for a piece of cheese. I

started to think about the possibility of failing that test. Wow, there were a lot of kids, and the halls were even more chaotic than the office.

Luckily, my safety-patrol training kicked in, and I was off like a rocket, dodging and weaving through the masses. I avoided swinging locker doors, bent-over shoe-tiers, scattered books, and slow-moving groups of gossiping girls. Guided by this sixth sense, I effortlessly made it to my classroom like some sort of hallway ninja. Who's better than me?!

Out of the corner of my eye, I saw a line of kids fast approaching. The lead kid was holding a sign: I BELONG TO MRS. WILLIAMS. Perfect!

The sign seemed STRANGE, but I made it. First mission: accomplished. I quickly jumped in line with the others and entered the classroom.

As usual, I headed straight to the back to keep a low profile. No need to draw attention to the new kid. I saw the hooks and hung up my backpack on the wall. Surveying the classroom, my first impression was that they sure made 'em small in Maryland. Compared to the other kids, I was a giant.

*Note to self: Don't drink the water!*

*Second note to self: Sign up for basketball tryouts immediately.* I saw total domination in my future!

Wanting to make a fantastic first impression, I marched up to the teacher and introduced myself.

"Hello, Mrs. Williams!" I said confidently. "I'm Jake, nice to meet you."

"Hello . . . Jake?" she answered, looking confused.

Handing her my "new kid" slip of paper, her confusion turned to anger.

"I'm so sorry! Welcome, welcome! You'd think the front office would let me know when I have a new student," she said. "Take any open seat and I'll be right back. Class, please make Jake feel welcomed!" she requested before leaving.

Considering what I'd witnessed earlier in the front office, I didn't think too much about her not expecting my arrival. As she exited the classroom, I felt an ocean of eyes upon me. Everyone was smiling and waving . . . WEIRD!

WHO WOULDN'T LOVE THESE SMILING FACES?

As I plopped down in a chair, my knees slammed into the attached desk. OUCH!! That's a tight fit. No more cookies for me!

It was the smallest desk EVER! I had to slump down really low to stretch out my legs, and my knuckles almost touched the ground. I felt like Buddy from the movie *Elf*.

"What's *Elf*?" you ask. Only the funniest movie of all

time. A true classic! When you see Buddy in class with the other elves, you'll think of me for sure!

With all the kids still staring at me, it was time to grab my backpack from the wall and find some distractions to escape that awkward silence.

I jumped to my feet, or at least that's what I tried to do. Unfortunately, the desk had other ideas. It clung to my body like an annoying piece of tape, and down I went. As I crashed to the floor, horrifically tangled in the desk/chair contraption, all I could think of was the importance of first impressions.

Instantly, I was surrounded by kids. But, instead of belly laughter and ridicule, the group quickly had me extracted from the Desk of Death.

Back on my feet and towering over my new friends, I was suddenly hit with a feeling of horror as the group burst into song:

"EVERYONE NEEDS A HELPING HAND,
A HELPING HAND, A HELPING HAND,

EVERYONE NEEDS A FRIEND WHO CARES,
WITH HELPING HANDS, A FRIEND WHO CARES,

JAKE NEEDS FRIENDS WHO CARE, WITH HELPING
HANDS, FRIENDS WHO CARE."

What the heck was going on?! Where was I? The Land of Oz? Something was not right.

When they finished singing, all the kids started jumping up and down and wildly shaking their arms over their heads. Nobody said a word. Just lots of smiles and this crazy arm-waving.

— — — — — — — —

The strange silence was broken by a loud clapping sound. I turned around to see Mrs. Williams in the doorway. She was beaming ear-to-ear.

"That was an excellent silent cheer, children! BRAVO! BRAVO!" shrieked the teacher.

Mrs. Williams motioned for me to join her in the doorway. As I walked over, all the kids patted me on the back and dusted me off. That fail was beyond epic.

The teacher, trying to control her laughter, told me I was in the wrong class. Apparently, there were two teachers at Kinney Elementary named Mrs. Williams: the Mrs. Williams who taught sixth grade, where I SHOULD have gone, AND Mrs. Williams the second-grade teacher.

Did that really just happen?

I closed my eyes, hoping I would wake from the nightmare. Sadly, there was no alarm clock. *OUCH!*

# CHAPTER 8
# BACK TO EARTH

Peeking into my REAL classroom, I quickly saw my basketball dreams shattered. Oh well, back to being below-average size. BUT I'm still GIGANTIC in AWESOMENESS.

## RULES OF AWESOMENESS #4

IF YOU BELIEVE IT TO BE TRUE, THEN IT IS. WARNING: THIS RULE ONLY APPLIES TO AREAS OF SELF CONFIDENCE AND THE QUESTIONING OF ONE'S SELF WORTH. IT DOES NOT APPLY TO GRADES, ATHLETIC ABILITY, OR RELATIONSHIP STATUS. (E.G., BELIEVING MOLLY SIMONE IS YOUR GIRLFRIEND DOES NOT MAKE HER YOUR GIRLFRIEND. IT MAKES YOU DELUSIONAL AND POTENTIALLY A STALKER!)

The two Mrs. Williamses needed a moment. As they

whispered quietly, I stood at the door anxiously awaiting instructions. Leaning toward each other, both teachers were trying to control their giggles.

Okay! Was I the first kid to ever make a mistake? *Grow up, ladies!* Also, enjoy it while you can. That will be my last blunder.

Second-grade Mrs. Williams was still cracking up as she left the classroom. *SERIOUSLY?* The real Mrs. Williams promptly introduced me to my new classmates. No smiles. No warm greetings. Just grumpy stares. Wow, I really missed the little guys and their silent cheering. The new group had real ATTITUDE!

Sitting down in the only open seat, I was greeted by a familiar face.

"Hey, man, WELCOME! Remember me? Jason? Jason Jackson? From across the street," said the same BIG kid who narrowly avoided becoming roadkill at the hands of Alexis the Terrible.

"Oh yeah! Hi! I'm Jake. YOU'RE in sixth grade?!" I asked, not really thinking that my utter amazement at this giant actually being in my grade could be considered insensitive.

I mean, this kid was HUGE. He wore an extremely loud neon-striped Volt shirt and had flowing blond hair that curved down in front of his eyes. You know the type. He looked exactly like the rich kid in any Disney Channel show.

The kid everyone loves to hate.

"YUP! I've been held back a few times," said Jason proudly. "Was that your sister with you the other day? MAN!!!!!! She's HOT!"

"Ah, yeah. That's my sister . . . 'HOT'?? I can think of a lot of words to describe Alexis, but HOT wouldn't be one," I said.

Hot-tempered, of course. Hot under the collar, for sure. Hot from volcanic anger building inside her? DEFINITELY. "Hot" as in very good-looking and cute? I didn't see it.

"ALEXIS!!!! Great name. WOW!! What grade is she in?" Jason asked, turning completely around and leaning on my desk.

"She's in eighth grade. Way too old for you. Besides, she's probably going to beat the crap out of you next time she sees you," I reminded the now-drooling Jason.

*DUDE!!! Not on my desk!*

"No biggie. You got to tell her I have a late birthday, and like I said, I've been held back a few times," said Jason.

# RULES OF AWESOMENESS #5

WHEN TRYING TO IMPRESS A GIRL, IT'S BEST NOT TO
REMIND HER HOW STUPID YOU ARE.
WE LIVE IN A HIGHLY COMPETITIVE GLOBAL ECONOMY. BEING
A BIG, DUMB JOCK IS UNFORTUNATE. BEING PROUD OF THIS
FACT JUST MAKES YOU A DUMBER VERSION OF YOURSELF.

"SUUUUURE! I'll let her know," I said.

"Dude, does she have a boyfriend?" Jason continued.

BOYFRIEND? I couldn't even imagine how unlucky
that guy would be. Wait a minute! Sure I could. I think a
typical Alexis/boyfriend convo would go like this;

> Boyfriend: "Hi, honey, I have a surprise for
> you. Check out this delicious box of chocolates.
> Sweets for my sweetie!"

> Alexis: "WHAT!? Are you trying to KILL me?
> Don't you know I'm in the middle of my lacrosse
> training package? I need to run two miles in
> under thirteen minutes. YOU IDIOT! Thanks for
> the extra sugar, fat, and calories."

> Boyfriend: "Ah . . . Um . . . Gee . . . I'm sorry?"

Alexis: "You should be sorry. Now go get me an asparagus smoothie. MORON!"

"Nope. No boyfriend. She is one hundred percent available," I said.

"Sweeeeet! Thanks for the info, BRO," Jason said as he swung back around in his chair. Although our talk was brief, there was something about that kid I instantly disliked. BRO?

Yeah, bro, good luck with Alexis, I thought. I just want to be there when you ask her out.

**JASON**

**KINNEY COLLECTION**

NICKNAME: BROSEPH
POPULARITY RANK: 10
NATURAL GIFT: HAIR FLIPPING AND CONFUSED LOOKS
411: STILL CAN'T COUNT WITHOUT USING FINGERS
SUCCESS?: YES! PATENT FOR USING ONE'S BODY TO SOLVE MATH PROBLEMS

Before I had time to imagine how mad Alexis was going to be when I told her about her new stalker, the bell rang.

*Look out!* These kids hustled!

A stampede of kids rushed the door. Caught in the flow, I was swept out with the mass migration of scrambling students.

Not knowing where to go, I followed the geekiest kid I could find. If I wasn't in his class, I should have been.

As expected, my man with the scientific calculator and holstered stainless steel compass led me to gifted math. I jumped into the first empty seat, but the teacher didn't even notice me.

THE SUM OF THE SQUARES OF THE TWO LEGS OF A RIGHT TRIANGLE IS EQUAL TO THE SQUARE OF THE HYPOTENUSE.

Hello! New guy here . . . I was about to get up and introduce myself when the teacher approached my desk with a big smile. FINALLY! Someone was going to make me feel welcomed.

WHACK! The teacher slammed a piece of paper down on my desk and kept walking. No greeting. No introduction. I looked down to see CHAPTER 5 TEST.

Next thing I heard was, "READY! Three, two, one . . . begin!"

What?!! Hang on! There must be some kind of mistake.

It's an unwritten rule of being the new kid . . . NO tests, NO quizzes, NO papers, NO projects! NO anything for at least two weeks. That teacher must have been new or a substitute. Time for action.

I approached her desk with my hand extended in an extremely polite formal introduction. I could see from her face Mrs. Tough Lady wasn't the warm, welcoming type.

"Good morning," I said in a whisper. "I'm Jake. The NEW kid."

"Shhhh! Back to your seat," hissed Mrs. Tough Lady.

"Oh, no, no . . . this is my first day. Are you a substitute?" I asked harmlessly.

———————————————————————

"No. I'm Mrs. Stone. AND I know who you are . . . JAKE from Florida," she said with extra emphasis on the *Jake*. "Now, go back to your seat and show me what you know."

*Houston . . . we have a problem.* UNHEARD OF!!!! It was an outrage. In the entire history of elementary school, no new kid was EVER asked to take a test on his first day. She was breaking a sacred, time-honored regulation of the Kid Constitution. (And if there isn't one, let's make one!) How is that fair?

*This is my first day of school in your lousy state, and you ask me to take a TEST!*

Mrs. Tough Lady, oh, sorry, Mrs. STONE, didn't care. She just shooed me back to my seat, like I was some peasant bothering the queen. You have to understand, I took great pride in my grades, and I was very scared that my first test-taking experience was not going to go well.

## RULES OF AWESOMENESS #6

MAKE IT YOUR MISSION TO ACHIEVE ACADEMIC EXCELLENCE. SCHOOLS AND YOUTH SPORTS ARE TRYING TO DO AWAY WITH IDENTIFYING WINNERS AND LOSERS, BUT LIFE HAS NOT. WE LIVE IN A SOCIETY WHERE TEACHERS ARE NO LONGER ALLOWED TO GIVE FS, AND EVEN THE LAST-PLACE TEAM GETS A HUMONGOUS TROPHY. THIS DOESN'T BEAR THE SLIGHTEST RESEMBLANCE TO ANYTHING IN REAL LIFE. CLASSROOM EXCELLENCE IS THE BEST WAY TO PREPARE FOR YOUR FUTURE.

Not recognizing any of the material on the test, it didn't take me long to finish. Can you say "Big Fat F"? I sat there in stunned silence. Before I knew it, Mrs. Stone was racing around the classroom, snatching the papers off everyone's desk. The bell rang and it started to feel like I was in a boxing match. Heading into round two!!

# CHAPTER 9
## I KEEP TRYING!

The rest of that day was more of the same. Only one teacher actually acknowledged my presence. To make matters worse, my two favorite periods, lunch and recess, were complete busts. Not one kid talked to me, and I ended up sitting by myself and keeping my head down, pretending to read a book.

Was I making an effort? Not really. But please don't judge me. It was a rough day. I really could have used some AWESOMENESS . . . But, oh well, it takes time to warm up.

My parents were devastated to hear that my first day

was the opposite of AWESOME. Of course, I added some stuff that didn't really happen. I needed to amp up the sympathy for a shot at double dessert!

Unlucky for me, though, my biggest detractor, Alexis, had a wonderful first day. Why unlucky? Because her no-drama, smooth-as-silk transition put the spotlight on me—the spotlight of SHAME!

"Don't worry, Jake, put today in your rearview mirror and look forward to being upbeat and positive tomorrow," suggested Mom. "It can only get better."

"Well, technically, Jake did screw up royally," Alexis added. "You only get one chance to make a first impression. From what I heard, the school's first impression of Jake is that he's a desk-crashing second-grade wannabe. OUCH! THAT HURTS!!!!" Alexis said, smelling blood and enjoying my misery.

"Jeez, Jake, what WERE you thinking?" asked Dad. "Didn't the kids look really young? Even in stressful situations, you need to maintain your perception."

"Exactly, Dad! Perception. Jake REALLY needs to up his perception game. How could a kid with so much talent and 'AWESOMENESS' lack this basic cognitive component?" Alexis added in a most concerned, grown-up tone, shaking her head and smiling.

"That's enough, Alexis," said Mom.

"No problem, Mom," I said. "She's right. I can't believe that happened to me. Now I know exactly how Alexis felt that time in Florida when she came out of the surf without her bikini top on. Or that time when she 'forgot' to pay for the soda at the convenience store, and the clerk threatened to call the police. Exactly right, Alexis! Maintaining one's perception is critical."

WHOOPS!

The bathing-suit incident they knew about. Who didn't? It happened during her class trip to the beach. The soda and the potential arrest were new info. I saw the spotlight of SHAME shifting to my adorable sister. Mess with the bull, you get the horns.

# RULES OF AWESOMENESS #7

ALWAYS KNOW YOUR OPPONENT'S STRENGTHS AND
WEAKNESSES.
INFORMATION IS THE KEY TO LIFE. BUT MORE IMPORTANTLY,
HOW YOU USE THAT INFORMATION TO GET YOURSELF OUT
OF TROUBLE IS CRITICAL. WHEN YOU'RE BEING ATTACKED,
HARNESSING THE ABILITY TO HOLD BACK PARTICULARLY
DAMAGING TIDBITS OF INFO UNTIL JUST THE RIGHT
MOMENT WILL BE THE DIFFERENCE BETWEEN GREATNESS
AND AWESOMENESS.

Do you have any idea what it's like being told over
and OVER, "You need to make an effort," or "You're better
than that," and, my personal favorite, "It's always darkest
before the dawn"? What does that even MEAN!? Darkest?
There's nothing dark about the spotlight of SHAME! It's
like looking into the SUN of DISAPPOINTMENT!

The next morning, my mom drove me to school again.
But this time, I insisted she drop me off in the parking lot.
No need for a grand entrance, considering my monumental
first-day fail.

Slipping in through the side door, I made it to my

locker without following any kindergartners to naptime. I was off to a good start.

Unfortunately, day two wasn't any better than day one. Now, you'd think a kid as wildly creative and outgoing as me could never be pegged as a social outcast. Think again. Actually, it was easy—all I had to do was transfer to a school where every kid had known every other kid since they could crawl. Not many new students ever show up at Kinney Elementary. It's a rare occurrence, like a Bigfoot sighting. Oh, forgive me, I meant to say *Sasquatch*.

YOU TALKIN' TO ME!?

BTW . . . have you ever watched the TV show where there's a bunch of guys searching for Bigfoot? It is HILARIOUS! These guys must have a million bucks worth of high-tech equipment, spend hundreds

of days in bug-infested forests, and they never come close to even seeing Bigfoot. Hey, fellas! Want to know why you haven't seen him yet? BECAUSE HE DOESN'T EXIST!

YES, I DO.

---

How about being the son or daughter of a professional Bigfoot hunter? That's got to be MUCH worse than being the new kid at Kinney Elementary. Just imagine the abuse those kids get:

"Hey, Jake, I saw your dad on TV. *Reaaalllly* cool show. He came *sooooooooo* close to catching that elusive Bigfoot," says the school bully.

"Shut up, jerk! My dad's the best dad ever," I say. But inside, I think my dad's losing it and needs Bigfoot therapy.

"Ooookay, Jake. When your dad does find Bigfoot, can I get an autograph? Not your dad's, of course! Bigfoot's autograph! I need it for my collection. I already have the Abominable Snowman's, Santa Claus's, and the Tooth Fairy's," says the bully.

I pretty much walked and talked to myself the whole day. Racing to and from my new classes, I didn't have much time to meet anyone. Lunch was the best opportunity. "Friend finding" was at the top of my list. I couldn't face the glare of the spotlight of SHAME once again.

My strategy was simple—befriend a kid at one of the low-ranking outer tables. After that, quickly move my way up the ranks to the more-popular inner tables. I figured it should take me about a week to pull that off.

## RULES OF AWESOMENESS #8

PLAN, MAN! DON'T BE A FAILURE.
LIFE IS LIKE A GAME OF CHESS: YOUR ABILITY TO PLAN, STRATEGIZE, AND SCHEME WILL SAVE YOUR KINGDOM. IN MIDDLE SCHOOL, THERE CAN ONLY BE ONE KING. IF YOU WANT IT TO BE YOU (NATURALLY YOU DO—SEE RULES OF AWESOMENESS #1), YOU BETTER PUT DOWN THE XBOX CONTROLLER AND START PLANNING YOUR ROAD MAP TO THE TOP. IF NOT, PREPARE TO BE ROUTINELY STUFFED INTO A LOCKER, AND BE READY TO ACCEPT THAT YOUR SEAT ON THE BUS WILL BE DIRECTLY BEHIND THE DRIVER.

Eyeing my first ~~victim~~ friend, I approached him with confidence. He looked harmless. Giving one of my best "tough guy" nods, I sat down across from him. Before he could say a word, I extended my hand for a formal introduction.

"Hey! How are you? I'm Jake!" I announced enthusiastically. It should also be noted I had an extra-giant chocolate-chip cookie in my other hand. Sliding it across the table to Friend #1, he took the bait. Never hurts to have a little insurance to make sure a plan goes smoothly. Some call it bribery . . . but not me. I call it AWESOMENESS IN ACTION!

Giving a far less "tough" nod, Friend #1 slowly raised his hands from his lap. He quickly placed a pile of green yarn and giant needle thingies on the table. I was stunned. *What's he DOING? I've seen this stuff before, but NEVER in school.* I got an immediate flashback to my grandmother's house. *Is this guy knitting? COME ON!!!!*

Yes, he was indeed KNITTING! Knitting Boy quickly scooped up his equipment and got back to work without saying a word. All I heard was the clicking and clacking of the knitting needles. Knitting Boy was in the ZONE! The yarn sped through his needles like bullets through a machine gun. Whatever he was making, he was following the directions from a magazine placed next to his half-eaten sandwich.

*Creative Knitting for Your Pet* might be a best-selling magazine in the knitting community, BUT it was probably not a smart choice to read during elementary-school lunch.

Knitting Boy didn't seem to notice me staring at him. Maybe he noticed my jaw smacking the floor? But I had no time to get to the bottom of all this knitting business, because my sister's future husband, Jason Jackson, immediately joined us.

"My man, Jake! What are you doing?" screamed Jason as he walked up and kicked Knitting Boy's left sneaker. "You definitely don't want to be eating lunch with old Norm here.

"Right, NORM?" Jason crowed loud enough to be heard by everyone. "You're an old lady trapped in a wimp's body!"

"Be careful, Jason. If you're not nice to me, I won't knit you that scarf you asked for," Norm replied.

"You're such a geek!" Jason screamed as he turned and walked toward the popular kids' table.

"There goes your scarf. Care to lose those mittens, too? You silly kitten!" Norm laughed.

*Wow! You go, Knitting Boy. Way*

I LOVE YOU.

to flip the script on Jason.

Although I had a newfound respect for Norm, I was still not going to sit with him. Though, considering Maryland is much colder than Florida, I could have really used a new scarf!

AND no way was I going to hang around with Jason the Jerk, either. My quest for a friend continued . . .

# CHAPTER 10
# RANKING SYSTEM

I took my parents' advice and gave my new school "time." Time to get used to the kids. Time to get settled in. Time to make friends and bring my unique form of AWESOMENESS to this Bumpkinville, USA.

After three months of "time," I was definitely ready to say I absolutely HATED my new school—and MARYLAND!

It was time to say *adios* and get the Big Guy to move back to sunny, FRIENDLY Florida.

I'm no quitter! BUT . . . you have no idea how bad it was. To have popularity suddenly ripped from my hands was hard to take. I was THE MAN in Florida. In Maryland,

NICK

**KINNEY COLLECTION**

NICKNAME: POSITIVE BOY
POPULARITY RANK: 5
NATURAL GIFT: FINDS SILVER LINING ANYWHERE
411: TIME WARP'S TWIN BROTHER
SUCCESS?: YES! MAKES LEMONADE OUT OF LEMONS.

my popularity fell off a cliff and sank to the bottom of the ocean. I had to do all my group projects with girls, and I didn't have anyone to sit with on the bus.

I only had one semifriend. His name was Nick, and he occasionally sat with me at lunch. When I could stand him. Which wasn't often.

I called him Positive Boy. Here's a typical conversation between us:

"Grand greetings, Jake! How are you on this most wonderful of days?" asks Positive Boy.

"Dude, it's raining outside! We also have a math test next period. So, I'm doing AWFUL!" I say in my most annoyed tone.

"I know! I studied all night. Super ready to ace the test. We'll both do fantastic! It's all good in the gifted-and-talented hood!" says Nick.

"Lacrosse is canceled, which means my mom will make me practice the piano tonight—which I HATE," I say.

"At least the trees and grass are getting life-sustaining $H_2O$—which reminds me, my mom packed some extra cookies," says Positive Boy.

"Cool. I'll trade you a granola bar for the cookies," I offer.

"Trade? You keep that granola bar. Remember, Jake, it's always darkest before the dawn," says Nick as he gives me a big bag of cookies.

NO!!!! Not him, too. I really need to find out what this whole "dark/dawn" thing is all about. Who talks like this?

I don't think you understand the severity of my

situation! I was less popular than Knitting Boy. Since his confrontation with Jason, he actually had a few friends. CRAZY! Didn't they see him KNITTING? Was I the only one with eyes? Man, Maryland was WACK! But before you suggest I take up knitting, need I remind you of my natural AWESOMENESS?

Unfortunately, it's taking a bit longer than usual to kick in. Was it me? Maybe I was trying too hard? Or not hard enough? This was a REAL problem. I'm Jake Ali Mathews; this doesn't happen to me. I had sailed into the uncharted waters of the Sea of Self-Doubt. WHY!!???

Without trying at my old school, I was a solid seven or eight on the popularity scale. That was WITHOUT trying. Factor in my academic success—I was in all advanced classes—and my ranking was through the roof, even with the burden of being brilliant. You know, the expectations . . . the pressures . . . the ability to read minds. Ha-ha! That's a joke. Just making sure you're paying attention.

Like I said, under normal circumstances, I'm a solid

seven or eight in popularity rank. Considering I've been to four elementary schools, I know what I'm talking about. Basically, every school has a ranking system. Start with the athletes, pretty girls, and rich kids, who mostly all rank between eight and ten.

The troublemakers, clowns, and cooler smart kids rank five through seven. As you start working your way down toward the bottom of the food chain, you'll find the brainiacs, freakazoids, lone wolves, and those with a passion for their grandmothers' hobbies.

Every so often, you'll encounter a kid that doesn't fit into any group. For some inexplicable reason, that kid is ranked off the charts in popularity. At Kinney Elementary, there was only one student like this—remember Camo Kid? I saw him on the first day of school. Well, come to find out, everyone at school knew him as WILD BOY. I'd say his popularity rank was a twelve. His fear rank was a twenty!

Wild Boy certainly lived up to his name. He wasn't much bigger than most kids in school, but he had huge muscles and slicked-back hair. He looked like a mini bodybuilder. Maybe he really should have been in high school? I doubt anyone would dare ask.

Also, he loved wearing tank tops. Even in the middle of winter. It could be twenty degrees outside with a foot of snow on the ground, and Wild Boy would STILL wear his camouflage pants and tank top.

Did I mention his tattoo? YUP! That's right! You heard it here first—sixth-grader gets tattoo. And not just any tattoo. Wild Boy's shoulder tattoo says BORN TO RAISE HELL. I couldn't make this stuff up if I tried. Is that even legal?

The rumor around school was that Wild Boy did the tattoo himself. That would make him INSANE! *Thank you, Dad, for moving me to Maryland! I do so love it here . . .*

## RULES OF AWESOMENESS #9

TATTOOS ON A TWELVE-YEAR-OLD ARE A REALLY BAD IDEA. A TATTOO IS PERMANENT! AS IN FOREVER! WHEN I WAS SIX YEARS OLD, I LOVED BUZZ LIGHTYEAR. NOW THAT I'M TWELVE, I'D LOOK REALLY STUPID ROCKING A GIANT BUZZ TAT ON MY ARM. "TO INFINITY AND HUMILIATION!"

Once word got back to the principal about Wild Boy's tattoo, you'd think he'd robbed a bank—which I definitely saw in his future. The police were called, and Wild Boy's father had to come to school for a "meeting." Can you say Father of the Year!?

My class was outside playing four square when Wild Boy's father arrived. He screeched across the parking lot in his jacked-up pickup truck. Let's just say, the apple doesn't fall far from the crazy tree!

It was crystal clear where Wild Boy got his style sense. After Wild Dad illegally parked across two handicapped spots, he exited his vehicle dressed in head-to-toe camo. Flicking his cigarette to the ground before strolling through the front door, Wild Dad didn't look too happy.

The next day, Wild Boy returned to school as if nothing happened. Apparently, because Wild Boy gave himself the tattoo, his parents weren't guilty of anything . . . besides not monitoring their son's behavior!

I can't wait to get a look at Mrs. Wild Boy. Hey, Mom, I have a new friend for you!

# CHAPTER 11
# THE REAL WILD BOY

Slowly but surely, life for me at Kinney Elementary improved. Starting with a popularity rank of zero, I knew things could only go up. After four long and painful months, I'd say I had reached a ranking of two, thanks to a lot of cookies and my intense studying of the Baltimore Ravens. For my football homework, I discovered the school's library technician, Mrs. Turlington, to be an unlikely expert.

After I first arrived and didn't have much luck making friends, I'd hide out in the library at lunch. Anything was better than sitting alone on LOSER ISLAND or listening to Positive Boy.

I think Mrs. T. figured out I was having a hard time, and she took pity on me. She's so COOL! She gave me all the Ravens' press guides and game programs, and even e-mailed me the team's weekly injury report. I eventually found out that she and her husband were season-ticket holders. Real Ravens fanatics. And, YES, I hate to say it, they were FACE PAINTERS!!! NO!!!!!!!!!

Even though face painters are the scariest of all crazy fans in the world of sports, Mrs. T. is still the most chill lady at Kinney Elementary. She armed me with mad Ravens knowledge, and before I knew it, I was talking about Ray Lewis and Joe Flacco, and questioning Coach Harbaugh's play calling every Monday morning on the bus.

RAY LEWIS IS A FIRST BALLOT HALL OF FAMER.

NO DOUBT.

Being buddies with Mrs. T. also meant she would hook me up with new books and passwords to all the latest and coolest websites. I became one of her "testers." If I liked something, the rest of the students would get it. This also helped me meet new kids, as everyone wanted to "borrow" my top-secret clearance.

I was truly on a popularity roll. Nowhere near Florida levels, but at least I had cleansed myself of the dreaded "new kid" stench that had lingered far too long.

With my confidence booming, it was time for a bold move. I had lots of acquaintances, but no real friends. Wild Boy didn't look like he had any friends, either. Perfect. It was time for AWESOMENESS to be formally introduced to CRAZY!

Wild Boy never played four square or basketball at recess, just mostly walked among the narrow line of trees at the edge of the parking lot. Not enough space to hunt for anything cool like elk or elephants, but it looked like he was always looking for something. One afternoon I made the mistake of venturing over and introducing myself.

"What's up? Looking for snakes?" I asked in my coolest, deepest voice.

Wild Boy was shocked. Was there some rule he wasn't to be disturbed?

With a heavy sigh AND an EYE ROLL, he turned to look at me. YES, he EYE ROLLED ME. Didn't he know I had THE ONLY password to BigIQkids.com's secret game page? Apparently NOT!

"Ants," he replied, shaking his head and trying to ignore me.

"Fantastic! I LOVE ants! Mind if I help? Did you know some ants can lift up to fifty times their own body weight?" I said.

WHERE ARE WE GOING?

THE GYM.

"Really?" replied Wild Boy. "That's an unbelievable coincidence. So can I!"

Suddenly, I felt my feet leave the ground as I was scooped into the air and flung over the crazy ant collector's shoulder. Three or four giant steps later, I found myself awkwardly sitting in the nearest garbage can. With my knees inches from my face, I quickly realized I had reached a new low. HELP!

## RULES OF AWESOMENESS #10

KNOW WHEN TO WALK AWAY.
NOBODY LIKES DEFEAT, BUT IN YOUR CLIMB TO THE TOP,
THERE WILL BE SETBACKS. DON'T LET PRIDE OR EGO WRITE
A CHECK YOUR OWN PHYSICAL AND MENTAL ABILITIES CAN'T
CASH. NECK BRACES ARE NOT COOL!

It took a while to wiggle out of the can. Nobody came to help me—everyone was too busy pointing and laughing. Off to the library I went. I needed to escape the Kinney version of the spotlight of SHAME.

Walking into the media center, I saw Mrs. T. at her desk. She sensed a problem right away.

"Hi, Jake. Shouldn't you be at recess?" asked Mrs. T.

"Technically, yes. But, I don't know, sitting in a garbage can isn't my idea of fun and relaxation," I said.

"What?! Garbage can? Why were you sitting in a

garbage can?" asked Mrs. T.

"Not by choice. Wild Boy didn't want to share his ants," I answered, still brushing off candy wrappers and dust from my time in the can.

"You mean Michael? He did that to you? Don't worry, he's harmless. He wouldn't hurt anyone. Actually, he is a very nice young man," said Mrs. T.

As I said, I hold Mrs. T. in the highest regard, BUT . . . come on, NICE!?

"Mrs. T.!!!!!! With all due respect . . . Wild Boy is a bully and a MANIAC! He shouldn't be allowed to prowl the grounds and hallways of this fine academic institution. With that kid around, we are ALL in grave danger!" I said in total disbelief.

"Nooooooooo . . . you're wrong. He's just misunderstood. You'd be surprised. He's very polite, smart, thoughtful, and extremely disciplined. Do you know he trains four to five hours every day?" said Mrs. T.

"Trains? Trains at what? Assault and battery?" I said.

Mrs. T. looked clearly annoyed. "Nope . . . at this!" she said as she slowly reached into her drawer and slid a magazine across her desk to me.

On the cover of *Martial Arts America* was the kid who had just gently placed me in a garbage can. *ARE YOU KIDDING ME?*

Turns out MASTER Wild Boy is no JOKE. In the under-thirteen national rankings for Tang Soo Do, the Wild One is number one!

The magazine was filled with pictures of Wild Boy holding up these GIANT trophies and doing crazy flying kicks. The kind of stuff you see in movies.

"So, you see, Jake, if Michael was truly a maniac, he could have done a lot more than put you in a garbage can. He was probably just kidding around," said Mrs. T. with a smile. "You should try again to make friends. I know he's ALSO having a hard time."

Oh yeah . . . THAT's what I'm going to do! It's bad enough I live in pure terror of him, now I'm supposed to go and actively seek him out. NO THANK YOU!!!! My AWESOMENESS has its limitations.

"Wow . . . IMPRESSIVE. Okay, I understand. I'll do that," I said, lying through my teeth. And BTW, I love my teeth. I want to keep them.

"And, Jake, please don't tell any of the other students about this stuff. Michael is a very private person. I just wanted you to know," said Mrs. T.

"It's in the VAULT!" I said, locking my mouth with a fake key and pretending to throw it away.

# CHAPTER 12
# THE KINNEY
# COLLECTION

Along with my newly acquired local-sports knowledge and a whole bunch of hallway *hellos* and *what's ups*, I slowly began to find my way at Kinney Elementary.

I was no longer being picked last for kickball, and I FINALLY had a regular lunch table. I called it the Table of Misfit Toys.

The great thing about my table was that it provided SO much inspiration for my new Kinney Kid Card Collection. Allow me to introduce the starting lineup . . .

Eleanor Ellis is one of a kind. It's like being friends with your mom when she was a kid. Eleanor doesn't have a cell phone. She has never used the Internet and isn't allowed to watch the Disney Channel. Her favorite show is *Lost in Space*! I'd never heard of it. She lives in a time warp. Eleanor wears long, floral-printed dresses and gigantic bows in her hair. One day, she told us about a new TV show she's watching called *I Love Lucy*. Supposedly, the show is in black-and-white. What does that even look like????

**ELEANOR**

**KINNEY COLLECTION**

NICKNAME: TIME WARP
POPULARITY RANK: 5
NATURAL GIFT: LIVING IN THE PAST!
411: POSITIVE BOY'S TWIN SISTER (SHOCKER!)
SUCCESS?: YES! WILL WORK IN A MUSEUM

## BEN

### KINNEY COLLECTION

**NICKNAME:** Big Ben
**POPULARITY RANK:** 6
**NATURAL GIFT:** Acting like he's British
**411:** Decided in second grade to be british
**SUCCESS?:** YES! As a great actor!

## JOE

### KINNEY COLLECTION

**NICKNAME:** Average Joe
**POPULARITY RANK:** 5
**NATURAL GIFT:** Being average at everything!
**411:** Wears his hat backward
**SUCCESS?:** Moderate

# CHAPTER 13
# CRASH & BURN

Needless to say, with my growing popularity and my small (but awkward) group of buds, I didn't see the need to EVER say another word to Wild Boy. Too dangerous.

At lunch, Wild Boy always sat by himself eating his deer sandwiches in silence. I wasn't sure if he was the ultimate cool guy or the creepiest kid EVER. But I knew to stay out of his way. And I wasn't alone.

When Wild Boy walked down the hall, the kids parted like the Red Sea. And no one EVER made eye contact with him. You looked straight down at your shoes and walked away.

One day, as Wild Boy sat alone, munching on Bambi, I was enjoying some big-time nerd fun with the Misfits. Our latest obsession was paper airplanes. Every day, we'd design them, fly them, compete, trade, and argue about whose was the best. It was our little lunchtime thing: aerodynamic AWESOMENESS!

---

That day, it was my turn to go. Although I "found" my new design in a book supplied by Mrs. T., I failed to mention that to the others. Like my old lacrosse coach in Florida would say, "If you ain't cheatin', you ain't tryin'!"

The goal of the competition was simple: make a paper airplane that could hit the far wall in one toss. Bonus points were given if the plane landed in the drinking fountain. Up until then, no one had come close. It was my day to make history.

My strategy was to throw the plane high from a seated position and get lots of loft. If I could get it up near the ceiling, I thought my paper masterpiece would safely glide across the room and onto the germ-infested landing strip. After wetting my finger and checking for crosswinds—probably should've used some hand sanitizer—I was all set to launch.

Just like Joe Flacco, I let loose a mighty toss. My paper missile soared high into the air. But from the second it left my hand, I knew something was wrong.

Spinning uncontrollably, my plane began losing altitude immediately. I don't think the death spiral was what the designer had in mind.

Even as the plane came crashing back to earth, the thought of it hitting someone never crossed my mind. That is, until my paper missile landed in the middle of Wild Boy's open-faced deer sandwich.

In shock, I looked at my friends, not knowing what to do. White with fear, my posse of future engineers and software designers slowly got up and then bolted for the exit.

Like most animals after a successful hunt, Wild Boy did not appreciate his prey being disturbed. He grabbed my plane and scanned the lunchroom for the offending party.

Locking eyes with me, Wild Boy slowly got to his feet. Frozen with terror, I was praying for a simple return to the garbage can as the baddest sixth grader on the planet approached my now-empty table. *Come on, GUYS!!! A little backup?*

"Hi, there! Is this YOUR plane?" Wild Boy asked. "You know, it's rude to throw planes into other people's food. Cool design, though."

Still paralyzed by the thought of being scissor-kicked in the head, I couldn't say or do anything. However, he didn't appear to be angry with me.

"Mrs. T. says you're okay. So I guess I'm sorry for putting you in the trash can before. That was stupid," said an APOLOGETIC Wild Boy.

Ha! My AWESOMENESS was FINALLY kicking in!

And maybe, due to our brief encounter, some of my AWESOMENESS had rubbed off on Wild Boy. Considering my proximity to an extremely large lunchroom dumpster, you could not appreciate my relief at his coolness.

Before I said a word, Jason Jackson appeared out of nowhere. Shoving Wild Boy from behind, the much-bigger Jason snickered and pointed as Wild Boy slid across the floor.

"Hey, Wild Flower, you think you can pick on my BEST BRO, Jake?" Jason yelled as he looked at me, smiling, winking, and acting like a complete idiot.

Unfortunately for Jason, I had kept my promise to Mrs. T. Nobody knew about Wild Boy's secret pastime.

"Whoa, whoa . . . WHOA THERE, JASON!! Everything

is fine. Michael and I were just talking . . . ," I said as I tried to diffuse the situation.

"Jake, I understand. DON'T WORRY! This kid isn't going to bully you anymore. Or anyone else at this school. Isn't that right, 'Michael'?" Jason said as he turned back to face Wild Boy.

"You want a piece of me, jerk?" Wild Boy asked in a very calm and deliberate tone.

"I don't want a piece of you, Wild Flower. I want the WHOLE THING!" Jason said as he inched closer to Wild Boy, poking him in the chest.

OHHH NOOOO!!!!!! Cell-phone cameras were at the READY! This was going to be YouTube worthy.

At no point did Wild Boy lose his cool. He remained calm; he even smiled slightly. I expected a sudden explosion of fists, chops, and a few *hi-yaahs*! That didn't happen.

On his toes and looking very agile, Wild Boy resembled a mongoose circling a snake.

"I don't want to fight you, Jason. It wouldn't be fair. I'm afraid I will hurt you," said Wild Boy.

"HURT me? You don't have to worry about that, you camo-loving freakazoid. I'm going to crush you like a bug!" Jason laughed.

"Are you sure? You really want to fight ME? I DON'T want to fight you. Are we clear? YOU are the aggressor? YOU, Jason, have assumed all responsibilities for your actions and are fully aware of the consequences associated with combat?" Wild Boy asked. He sounded like one of the waivers you sign every time you visit an ultradangerous water park. Jason looked SO confused.

I didn't understand why Wild Boy just didn't start pounding on Jason. It was either a Jedi mind trick, or Wild Boy's training included a course in lawsuit prevention.

THIS ISN'T THE LAWSUIT YOU'RE LOOKING FOR.

"Are you nuts?! I'm going to freakin' shred you. Let's GO!!!!" Jason yelled as he put up his fists and started to move forward.

"Okay. I accept your challenge," Wild Boy said as he punched one of his fists firmly into the palm of his other hand, bowing quickly toward Jason. "But not in school. I know where you live. How about this Saturday, 5:00 p.m., your house?"

"Sure . . . you'll come to my house for a WHOOPIN'! Okay! Makes it easy for me," said Jason. "It's time I teach you the real law of the jungle, WILD CHILD!"

By this time, every kid at lunch was watching, and a giant "fight circle" had formed. Seeing the commotion, the teachers finally came running to investigate. Not wanting any trouble, the two gladiators quickly slipped back to their lunch tables.

After lunch I had to hit my locker to pick up books for English and history. Spinning the combination lock, I felt a tap on my shoulder. It was Jason, proudly nodding his head, smirking and offering up a congratulatory high five. UCK! I left him hanging.

"Hey, man, make sure you tell Alexis I had your back. I'm sure she'll love me for looking after her LITTLE BRO," said Jason.

"What was that all about?" I demanded. "TOTALLY unnecessary. I had it handled. There was no need for you to get involved."

"Dude!! Come on. You had nothing handled. Unless, of course, you were looking for Wild Boy to upgrade you into the lunchroom dumpster," Jason said with a laugh.

"Yeah right! That wasn't going to happen," I said. "Besides, Wild Boy wasn't mad at all, before you came over and stuck your nose . . ."

"MY MAN!" interrupted Jason. "You don't know this kid. HE'S CRAZY! I heard he got kicked out of his last school for bringing his pet rattlesnake in for show-and-tell."

"I'm pretty sure that didn't happen," I said.

"No, no, it did. You have no idea. He eats insects and even shaved a kid's head once. I'm telling you, he's no good," implored Jason.

## RULES OF AWESOMENESS #11

NEVER, EVER ARGUE WITH A COMPLETE IDIOT. THEY HAVE EXPERIENCE ON THEIR SIDE AND WILL BEAT YOU EVERY TIME. THERE ARE PLENTY OF IDIOTS OUT THERE. YOUR JOB IS TO IDENTIFY THEM AND STAY AWAY. ENGAGING THEM ONLY WASTES YOUR TIME AND MAKES YOU STUPIDER. I'VE FOUND THAT A DEEPLY THOUGHTFUL LOOK WITH CONSTANT NODDING (IN FAKE UNDERSTANDING) FOLLOWED BY AN ABRUPT "HOLD ON A SECOND, I'LL BE RIGHT BACK" IS THE ONLY WAY TO QUICKLY ESCAPE THE MENTAL CLUTCHES OF AN IDIOT.

Realizing I had very little time to get to my next class, I turned and ignored Jason's rambling and quickly finished my combination. Grabbing my backpack, I accidentally pulled the Kinney Collection out of my locker, spilling the crisply laminated cards all over the hallway.

OH NO!

Bending down to help, Jason picked up his buddy Garrett's card.

"What the heck is this?" Jason asked.

"Nothing. Just an art project I'm working on," I said, trying to find a reasonable excuse.

"Is that supposed to be Daniel?" asked Jason. "It looks NOTHING like him. 'Downtown'? That's not his nickname. We call him Swish!

DANIEL

KINNEY COLLECTION

NICKNAME: DOWNTOWN DANIEL
POPULARITY RANK: 10
NATURAL GIFT: SHOOTING CLUTCH 3's
411: HE HAS FOUR OLDER BROTHERS!
SUCCESS?: YES! NBA STAR FOR SURE

"Is THAT Paige? Oh my GOD! She's going to love her

## PAIGE

### KINNEY COLLECTION

NICKNAME: Posing Paige
POPULARITY RANK: 1
NATURAL GIFT: Being into only herself
411: Always ready for her close-up
SUCCESS?: Yes! In the mannequin business

nonexistent nose! How many of these things do you have?" asked Jason.

"Ah . . . not many, a few. It's kind of a hobby," I said.

"Man, you're kind of a weirdo," said Jason. "But I LIKE you. And your sister!"

Just then, the bell rang, and Jason dropped the cards and sprinted to his next class. I quickly collected the rest of the Kinney Collection and prayed Jason didn't fully understand what they were.

# CHAPTER 14
# LITTLE BRO'S BETRAYAL

LET'S GET READY TO RUMBLE!!!!!!!

The BIG FIGHT was all anyone talked about. Signs started appearing around school. Kids made strategic sleepover plans with friends who had COOL parents. You know the type: parents who really don't care what you do.

"Hey, Mom, me and Bobby are going outside to blow up my toy cars with all those firecrackers we bought in South Carolina," says Lucky Kid.

"Have fun, dear. Come home later for dinner if you want," says Coolest Mom on Earth.

"I don't think so. We're going over to watch

the big fight between Wild Boy and Jason. Won't be home until late," says Lucky Kid.

"Oh, great! I hope Jason wins," says Cool Mom.

In this case, I was kind of "lucky," because fight central was directly across the street from my house. Unlucky for me was the fact I had to see Jason every day that week.

Walking to the bus, walking from the bus, getting the mail, taking out the trash, riding my bike . . . the kid was everywhere! ALL he wanted to do was talk about Alexis! The only good thing was that he didn't have anything to say about the Kid Cards, which was great. Big, goofy Jason was obsessed with my sister. Finally!! Alexis was good for something!

His obsession became a constant annoyance. A day didn't go by without me hearing one of the following from Jason:

"Does she know about the big fight?"

"Did you tell her I protected you?"

"Can I get her number?"

"Does she want my number?"

"Did you remind her I should really be in eighth grade?"

I assured him Alexis was well-informed. Actually, the ONLY thing I told her was that Jason failed a bunch of grades. The other stuff . . . not so much. Why would I? If I told her anything that angered her, she might decide to kill the messenger.

All I wanted to do was get Jason to stop talking to me. The kid was superconceited. He only cared about his hair and trying to impress my sister. He had NO idea what was about to happen.

And, of course, being a man of my word, I couldn't tell him about Wild Boy's martial-arts mastery. Breaking a promise to Mrs. T. would show a lack of AWESOMENESS.

Yet, trying to keep a secret like that was tough. I felt like I was going to BURST. I had to tell someone! And Mom and Dad weren't "students."

Strolling into the kitchen that weekend, I saw my

opportunity. Mom was reading the paper, and I knew I'd have her undivided attention.

"Hey, Mom, I want to show you this video on YouTube," I said. "This kid at my school is some kind of sick martial-arts expert. Check it out."

As I propped up the iPad, Dad came in for his twentieth cup of coffee.

"What's going on here? Jake, don't you have homework?" asked Dad.

"Chillax, my man! It's Saturday. I have lacrosse practice this morning, and later today the Misfit Toys are all coming over. Sunday is for homework," I said. "Hey, don't go anywhere. You've got to see this."

I showed my parents a quick vid of Wild Boy smashing fools and hoisting championship trophies. They were both impressed.

"This 'Wild' kid goes to your school?" asked Dad,

pointing in bewilderment at the screen. "Stay AWAY from him. He looks like trouble."

Just then, my sister made her presence known.

"*Mmmmmuuuuuuuuuuurrrrrrgggggghhhhh!!!!!!!!!*" groaned Alexis as she shuffled into the kitchen. Never a morning person, that was her standard, cranky greeting. WOW . . . only 10:00 a.m., still WAY too early for Sleeping Beauty!

Walking like a zombie, and of course, clutching Mr. Chuckles, Alexis cleared the sleep from her eyes. You've got to love an eighth grader still snuggling up with her WITTLE TEDDY BEAR!!

Noticing my parents watching something intently on my iPad, Alexis very quickly

SAVE ME FROM THE EVIL CLUTCHES OF . . . OH, HI, ALEXIS.

snapped out of her sleepy stupor.

"What's going on? What did I miss? Who's THAT? Jake, you know this kid? Excellent form! Do you see how level his head is on that spinning back-fist? Bad a✗✗!" said Alexis, nodding her head in approval.

"ALEXIS! Watch your mouth. That language is not ladylike," shrieked Mom.

Oh, Mom! It's WAY too late to worry about ladylike behavior. That train left the station. It's rumbling down the tracks headed straight for "Bad-Girl-Ville." All aboard!

"Who's that kid, Jake?" Alexis demanded, now extremely interested.

"It's Wild Man!" shouted Dad, heading back to his office.

"WILD BOY! Get it right. And, yes, he goes to my school," I yelled.

"His parents must be very proud. He's such a little cutie!" said Mom.

"WAIT a minute! That's the kid fighting Jason the Genius." Alexis started to figure it out before I cut her off. Standing behind my mom, frantically jumping up and down, and making a pretend slash across my throat—even Alexis understood the international DO NOT TELL MOM AND DAD sign!

"What, dear? He's fighting OUR Jason? Across-the-street Jason?" asked Mom.

"NO!!!! They're buddies. They just like to spar with each other. It keeps Jason in shape for football," I said, knowing full well MOM was the last person who needed any details about that evening's main event.

"Sparring, huh? I heard they're supposed to 'SPAR' tonight," Alexis said with a laugh.

"Wonderful. That Jason is a nice boy," Mom said. "Well, see you guys later. I'm off to the mall. Enjoy the sparring!"

I poured myself some cereal. It was time for a TV break. Unfortunately, Alexis had beaten me to the couch and was already stretched out end-to-end enjoying her favorite show, *Gossiping Liars*.

Quickly referencing Rules of AWESOMENESS #10, I decided to head to the basement for some peace and quiet.

*DING-DONG!!!!!!* WOW . . . kind of early for visitors. Girl Scouts? Oh yeah! Thin Mints rule!

I bounded up the stairs and into the hallway hoping to buy a few boxes of deliciousness.

But instead of cute little kids trying to sell me fifty boxes of cookies, I saw Jason standing outside on our porch. I just couldn't stomach another second of this guy. But I knew someone who could!

"Alexis? Can you do me a HUGE favor?" I asked nicely.

"If you think I'm turning off *Gossiping Liars*, you're NUTS! Lizzy is about to tell Natasha that she is in love with Brogan!" screamed Alexis.

"Come on, just pause it for a minute. Jason from across the street is at the door, and I REALLY don't want to deal with him," I pleaded.

To my surprise, Alexis slowly picked up the DVR remote and hit Pause.

"Okay. THAT I can do," said Alexis. With a heavy sigh and a roll of her eyes, she got up off the couch.

"Whatever you do, don't tell him I'm here!" I whispered loudly.

"Yeah, yeah . . . I GOT THIS!" snapped Alexis.

With her hair up in a bun and still dragging Mr.

Jason
↓

Chuckles by his long, stretched-out arms, Alexis moved slowly toward the front door. ANNOYED!

Flinging open the door, Alexis was greeted by Jason slumped against the porch railing in his best "cool guy" lean.

"What the HECK do you want, dragon breath!?!" yelled Alexis.

———————————

"HEY, girl . . . what's up?! Is Jake home?" Jason asked innocently.

Watching the interaction from under the dining-room table, I could see Alexis's arm still wrapped around the inside of our front door. She started to give me the thumbs-up sign.

"LACROSSE!!!!" was Alexis's answer as she quickly slammed the door in Jason's face.

Alexis

Pleased with herself, Alexis started the long shuffle back to the couch. But she didn't get five feet until the unthinkable happened . . . *DING-DONG!*

Highly agitated, Alexis remembered her unfinished business with Jason. Maybe now was the time to finally introduce him to the cobra strike.

With her blood boiling and a slight twitch in her face, Alexis slowly opened the front door once again.

"Hey, babe, sorry, but do you know when he'll get back?" asked Jason. "I want to make sure he comes over early, around four, to help me prepare for the big fight."

"Right! The fight. You've accepted the role of Wild Boy's punching bag. What on earth would possess you to want to fight THAT kid? I know you're stupid and everything, but you must be a LOT dumber than you look," Alexis sneered as she gave Jason her best UNIMPRESSED face.

"Didn't Jake tell you?!" Jason asked.

"Tell me what, Einstein?" said Alexis. "That you failed about five grades? I know that."

"No!! Well, yeah, I wanted you to know that . . . It's ONLY two grades, NOT five!" corrected Jason. "The reason I'm fighting Wild Boy?? Don't you know??"

Alexis just stood there, staring at Jason.

"To protect Jake! Didn't Jake tell you?" demanded Jason. Again, nothing from Alexis. She continued to stare at Jason like he was an alien.

"Wild Boy was bullying him, so I stepped in. I got your little bro's back. Don't worry, I'm going to pound Wild Flower. Pretty cool, right!? And after, you know, maybe we can hang out?"

Alexis recoiled in horror. This was not the reaction Jason anticipated.

Stunned that he wasn't being smothered with kisses and *oh, my heros*, Jason started to feel betrayed. This feeling grew more intense as Alexis began belly laughing uncontrollably.

Wiping the tears of laughter from her eyes, Alexis gained her composure.

"Hang out with YOU!! Are you joking?! First, I don't 'hang out' with boys in grade school," Alexis said with a laugh. "Second, even if I made an exception, I don't think you'll be much fun to 'HANG OUT' with after tonight. It's REAL hard to dance in a full body cast."

BEFORE WILD BOY

AFTER WILD BOY

"What does that mean?" Jason demanded.

"How do you NOT KNOW?" Alexis continued. "Jake didn't tell you about Wild Boy?"

Jason's look of utter confusion answered that question. *I didn't see this coming! Please don't!*

"OH NO? Well, THAT'S not very nice. It appears my little bro neglected to inform you about Wild Boy being a nationally ranked martial-arts master," said Alexis. "That IS unfortunate. Do yourself a favor and Google 'Michael Boyd' and 'Tang Soo Do.'"

"Tang Soo what??" said Jason. "What are you talking about? I'm going to destroy that little freak."

"EARTH TO IDIOT! Wild Boy is an EXPERT in beating people up. He's ranked number one in the country in his age group. Look at the videos. He crushes guys twice your size. You CAN'T win," Alexis explained. "But . . . I wish you the best of luck. NOW, get off my porch before I beat Wild Boy to the PUNCH. Get it? 'PUNCH'! Of course you don't . . . TOO FUNNY!"

SLAM went the door once again.

As Jason ran home to his computer, he probably thought about when he first challenged Wild Boy in the lunchroom. The weirdness, the bowing, the "Are you sure YOU want to fight ME?" stuff. It all probably started to make sense.

Shuffling back to the couch, Alexis saw me still hiding

under the table. All I could do was hold up my hands and ask, "WHY?"

"WHAT!" Alexis snarled. "I did you a favor. Jason now thinks you're a backstabbing worm. He won't want to be your friend. You're WELCOME!"

"Yeah, no kidding. He won't want to be a friend, but he WILL want to kill me!" I yelled.

"Jake. You are MY little brother. If he even looks at you funny, I'll destroy him. I saw the fear in his eyes. He won't be bothering you," Alexis said calmly.

That made me feel a little better. But she didn't have to ride the bus with him every morning.

# CHAPTER 15
# THE BIG FIGHT

As soon as I got home from lacrosse practice, text messages from the Misfit Toys blew up my phone. The plan was on! Everyone was meeting at my house and then straight up to my bedroom to watch the fight.

Living across the street from Jason provided me with an unobstructed view of the field of battle. It was like having my own VIP skybox. AWESOME!

Donald was bringing his dad's new HD video camera, and Tommy and I were going to be the announcers. I told my mom we were working on a science project. And hinted that some of her famous popcorn would be MOST appreciated. Score! Livin' the DREAM . . .

Before I knew it, my street was a sea of kids. They came on bikes, Razor scooters, and RipStiks. Some even had their parents drop them off. They looked like a crowd of rowdy soccer hooligans.

DONALD III

KINNEY COLLECTION

NICKNAME: THE DONALD
POPULARITY RANK: 10—MONEY BUYS FRIENDS.
NATURAL GIFT: SPENDING HIS PARENTS' CASH
411: BUYS YOU ICE CREAM AT LUNCH!
SUCCESS?: YES! ALREADY WORTH MILLIONS!

As we munched on popcorn and drank very cold soda, I started to feel bad for Jason. Did he deserve what was about to happen to him? Not really. But then again, he brought it upon himself. All in the name of love! At 5:00 p.m. on the dot, Wild Boy appeared outside Jason's house. Just like in the hallways at school, the masses of kids stepped WAY back and created a clear path to Jason's front door.

Wild Boy showed no emotion.
Very businesslike. This was not
his first time at the butt-
kicking rodeo. And, of course,
he wore his favorite black
sleeveless shirt, showing off
his ridiculously intimidating
tattoo. Indeed, he was "born
to raise hell."

After a few minutes and
no Jason, the crowd started to
get restless. Wild Boy even went to the front door and
knocked! That took guts! Was he going to ask if Jason
could come out and play?

To everyone's surprise, Jason suddenly appeared in a
second-floor window. With tears in his eyes, he leaned out
and yelled at the crowd.

"I'm NOT coming out! Get outta here. Wild Boy wins!!"
Jason wailed as he slammed the window shut.

The stunned crowd of kids stood in silence. This was quickly followed by a chorus of laughter and everyone taking turns mocking Jason's dramatic announcement.

**BILLY**

**KINNEY COLLECTION**

NICKNAME: BIG BULLY
POPULARITY RANK: 9
NATURAL GIFT: BEING ANGRY ALL THE TIME!
411: CAN STUFF ANY KID INTO A LOCKER
SUCCESS?: MAYBE AS A BODYGUARD

Billy Regan did the best Jason impression. "I'm NOT COMING OUT!!!! Get outta here . . . YOU MEANIES," Billy repeated, stomping his feet and holding his breath until his face turned beet red.

Up in the skybox, my guests were at a loss for words. I breathed a sigh of relief. It was probably the smartest thing Jason ever did, even though his all-American cool-guy reputation died that day.

On Monday, his popularity ranking would fall to a never-before-seen low. If he was lucky, Knitting Boy might make some room for Jason at his table.

Pleased with my small role in the downfall of Jason, I enjoyed the rest of the night playing flashlight tag with the Misfits. Monday was going to be fun!

# CHAPTER 16
## PAYBACK

Fresh off the bus on Monday, I ran into school. And no, Jason didn't even look at me. Finally, I was sitting solo!

So many kids who couldn't make it on Saturday wanted to hear the story. It was the biggest news of the year. Eventually I would get sick of retelling it. But, realizing I still needed maximum time in homeroom to talk about the NONFIGHT, I sprinted to drop off my backpack.

As I rounded the corner to the sixth-grade hall, I saw Jason standing next to my locker. A lightning bolt of fear shot through my body. *Oh no! What does he want?*

Quickly regaining my composure, I remembered a lesson I learned from the Discovery Channel. When you come face-to-face with a wounded lion, never turn and run. However, in this case, running made perfect sense. If I ran fast enough, I could probably find Wild Boy. But hang on!!! I saw what happened on Saturday. There was nothing to fear. Sure, I'm no martial-arts expert, but then again, what's Jason going to do? Yell at me?!

With newfound bravery, I walked straight up to my locker, which was OPEN, and slammed it shut.

"What the heck do you want, Jason!?" I asked. "And stay out of my locker!"

"No problem, JAKE. But you're probably going to want these back," Jason said as he walked backward down the hall, holding up my box of Kid Cards.

*YIKES!!!! Not the KINNEY COLLECTION!!!!!!!*

My life flashed before my eyes. Calming down, I tried to reason with Mr. Jason.

"Hey, dude, you know that's my art project. Can I have

it back?" I asked meekly.

"Nope! These are too perfect. By the end of today, everyone will be talking about YOU . . . and NOT me!" he shouted, as he turned and raced to homeroom.

I was in SERIOUS TROUBLE! *What to do? What to do? . . .* I kept THINKING!!!! But I was getting no answers.

As the first bell rang, I followed Jason to homeroom. I needed to be smart. Who knows? Maybe he's just going to hold them for ransom? I thought maybe five dollars could get them back. Was I thinking irrationally? OF COURSE he wasn't looking for money. I knew exactly what he was going to do.

As I sat down, Jason was already sorting through the cards. He had an evil look in his eye. A look of revenge.

I made a quick move to grab the cards, but the kid was a giant. He just laughed and held the collection high above his head. The cards were out of reach, and I was out of luck.

Sitting back down, I tried once again to have a rational conversation.

"What's your problem, Jason?" I asked. "What did I do to you?"

"REALLY! What did YOU do? It's what you didn't do! You KNEW all about Wild Boy's crazy karate stuff!" shouted Jason. "That kid would have KILLED me! Thanks for the heads-up . . . NEIGHBOR!"

"Karate stuff??? What are you talking—?" I started to reply but was quickly cut off by an increasingly hostile Jason.

"DUDE!!!! Don't even try to lie about it!" Jason bellowed, shaking his head in disgust. "Your sister told me everything. Oh yeah, and thanks for NEVER telling her about me, either."

I certainly hadn't anticipated that reaction from Jason. It appeared that I had violated Rules of AWESOMENESS #7; I had drastically underestimated him and was about to pay the ultimate price.

It had taken me months of suffering through pride and swallowing self-doubt to finally make it back to the summit of Mount Popularity. With one spiteful act, Jason was about to send me on a nonstop sleigh ride back to Trash Bin Valley.

When the end-of-homeroom bell rang, Jason took off like a rocket. And it didn't take long to see his plan in action.

Walking to first period, I saw Jason way down the hall, darting from side to side. At every group of kids, he'd stop briefly, distribute some cards, and then be off. *Man, he's pretty quick for a big guy.*

There was absolutely nothing I could do. After math class, I bolted to science knowing PLENTY of kids had already seen my handiwork. The Kinney Collection DID include some slightly unflattering and borderline mean stuff. Remember, I was in a very dark place when I made most of those cards. *THIS IS NOT GOING TO BE GOOD!*

In a complete and utter panic, I ran into the principal's office. I kept trying to remember all the stuff I had written. Was there ANYTHING nice?

Principal McCracken was sitting in her chair, looking all frazzled and confused . . . as usual! The last thing this lady wanted was ANOTHER kid problem. Funny, she looked even more nervous to be in the principal's office than me.

---

"JAKE . . . why are you here? Pleeeasssssseee GO!" shouted Principal McCracken.

"Sorry! Can't do that. Life-or-death situation here. Jason stole my Kid Cards and is giving them out to the whole school," I blurted. "Now I face annihilation at the hands of my fellow classmates, so I'm here to—"

"NOT TODAY, JAKE!" interrupted the principal. "Don't you know it's MONDAY? I don't have any announcements written. I have Billy Benson's parents coming in about the 'accident' last week, and of course no one has the keys to the gym."

**BILL**

**KINNEY COLLECTION**

NICKNAME: Brainiac
POPULARITY RANK: 10 . . . Fun at Parties!
NATURAL GIFT: Combustion!
411: His dad's a fireman.
SUCCESS?: Yes! Already has two patents!

As she pushed me out the door, I felt like I was being fed to the wolves. Would the Misfit Toys abandon me? I wondered if Knitting Boy still had room at his table.

All eyes were on me. Which kid was going to punch me first?

"Jake! I LOVE my card," said Julie Jones. "Can you make my hair a TINY bit blonder?"

"Broseph . . . my picture is rockin'! But you need to AMP up my bio with some righteous factoids!" exclaimed Bobby Tomkins.

"Yeah, me too, Jake. You forgot to say I'm the president of the debate team," chimed in Lucy Smith.

OMG! Everyone knew my name. They LOVED the cards!? It took me a second to soak it all in. Jason's plan had worked, but not like he intended. Everyone certainly forgot about his screaming and crying fit. But revenge was NOT his. He was defeated by AWESOMENESS! The entire school was consumed with my Kinney Collection. In a good way! I was BACK ON TOP!!

All day, kids asked me about the cards. Some even wanted to know how to make their own cards. Before I knew it, I had a line of kids at my lunch table requesting their own cards or changes to the original.

"Make one of me, Jake. PLEASE!!! I need a card!" Susie Shoemaker pleaded.

_____

Everyone got in on the act. Kid Cards were hot. Silly Bandz kind of hot! I was going to be a MILLIONAIRE!

Soon, kids were trading the cards. I couldn't make them fast enough. But there was one card every collector wanted. The ORIGINAL Wild Boy card. I was sure to take that one out of circulation.

Turns out, Wild Boy finally decided he really didn't like eating alone. He dropped the whole "I'm about to kill you" look by trashing all his camo gear and cutting his hair. And his BIG BAD tattoo? A fake! Can you say Sharpie fine point?

Mrs. T. was right. He was a great kid. Wild Boy is now

known as "Michael," and he's pretty smart! He's currently being tested for the gifted program—go figure!

Check out his new look. But don't let the clean-cut, innocent little kid fool you . . . He's still a one-man wrecking machine. *Hi-yaah!!*

Thanks for reading about my life. In the end, all is STILL GOOD in the Kinney Elementary HOOD! And you know what? IT IS darkest before the dawn. Now I get it! Positive Boy was right!

# EPILOGUE
## UPDATE ON
# AWESOMENESS

Just in case some of you were concerned, I want to give you an update on my progress. Much like I predicted, after a few more months at Kinney Elementary, I was once again at Florida levels of AWESOMENESS. It felt so good to have my mojo back.

School's now a breeze! The weather warmed up, and the spring flowers are everywhere. Life is GREAT!

Michael, who is no longer "WILD" at all, is my best bud. Last weekend, he slept over and we planned on watching hours of college basketball. I finally showed Michael my Kid Card of him; we both laughed at how much he's changed.

Dad finally finished his "man cave," and we are about to test-drive his new high-definition projector.

Unfortunately, Alexis had also done well socially. Her new gang of overly huggy, drama-loving dorks invaded our house that night, and I knew she was going to try to evict me and Michael from the cave of giant-screen luxury.

"Hi, little bro!!! Why don't you and Wild Whatever run along upstairs? Mommy and Daddy want to watch Sesame Street with you two BIG BOYS," Alexis said with a laugh while her posse of brace-faced geeks giggled in the background.

"I don't THINK so. I'm waaayyyy too comfortable to go anywhere," I said, reclining even further in my dad's new chair.

"You won't be too comfy after I jump on your chicken chest and dance all over your spleen," said Alexis, who was still trying to maintain her smile.

Weighing my options, I didn't have a choice. Alexis knew Michael wouldn't do anything. Since his public humiliation of Jason, Michael had sworn to only use his super BUTT-KICKING powers to fight evil.

UNFORTUNATELY, being booted from the basement didn't qualify. Michael's inner Wild Boy remained dormant.

By myself, I didn't stand a chance. Alexis had been hitting the P90X really hard lately and was in full-blown beast mode. Better to run away and live to fight another day.

Furious, I motioned to Michael and we headed for the exit.

"That's right! Thanks for coming! See ya next time," crowed Alexis as we picked up our pillows, blankets, and snacks.

The laughter from her group of goofy hags grew louder as we climbed the stairs. Michael said nothing. What good is being a 2nd dan black belt in Tang Soo Do if you can't put it into action? Since his transformation into a gifted-and-talented nerd, he's turned into quite the wimp.

Alexis laughed the loudest. There was no doubt her special gift of MEANNESS had also followed her to

Maryland. But meanness is no match against extreme AWESOMENESS. Don't forget, Michael wasn't the only one with superpowers.

After closing the basement door, I told Michael to hold on, and I headed for my mom's office. Two of the great things about Mom are her attention to detail and her acute organizational skills. She is one of those moms who are always taking pictures of the family, especially us kids.

Every play, recital, game, and special moment, Mom was there, snapping away. I grew up with a camera in my face. And so did Alexis. Unfortunately for my big sis, she's just not as photogenic as I am.

Browsing the numerous bookcases full of photo albums, I took down a

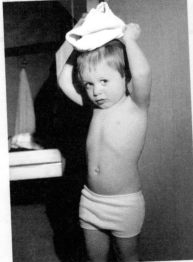

few of my personal favorites: "Alexis—Potty Success," "Alexis—Birthday (Grumpy, Grumpy)," "Alexis—First and LAST Ballet Lesson," and "Alexis—Cuts Her Own Hair"!

As I marched back downstairs with albums stuffed under each arm, I thought about my AWESOMENESS. Not so funny anymore, is it, Alexis? It's good to be Jake Ali Mathews. I am THE GREATEST!

THE VIRUS!

## SAM

### OCEANVIEW COLLECTION

**NICKNAME:** THE VIRUS
**POPULARITY RANK:** 3, BUT A 1 DURING FLU SEASON
**NATURAL GIFT:** HOSTING STRAINS OF FLU VIRUS
**411:** FUNNY THING IS, HIS MOM IS A NURSE.
**SUCCESS?:** YES! ODDLY GETS GOOD GRADES

# HAMMERIN' HANK

## HANK

## OCEANVIEW COLLECTION

**NICKNAME:** HAMMERIN' HANK
**POPULARITY RANK:** 9
**NATURAL GIFT:** SWALLOWING FOOD WITHOUT CHEWING
**411:** DON'T SIT NEAR HIM ON TACO TUESDAYS.
**SUCCESS?:** I HOPE SO. VERY LIKEABLE

# MINI BOLT

## SERGIO

### OCEANVIEW COLLECTION

**NICKNAME:** MINI BOLT
**POPULARITY RANK:** 8
**NATURAL GIFT:** FAST. ANNOYINGLY FAST
**411:** HE WINS ALL THE RACES IN GYM CLASS.
**SUCCESS?:** MAYBE. NOT SURE HE'S HUMAN

# ABOUT THE AWESOME AUTHOR

Jake Marcionette is a seventh-grader living with his mom, dad, and big sister in Florida. He wrote the manuscript for *Just Jake* when he was just twelve years old. In addition to writing, Jake loves playing lacrosse and annoying his sister, Alexis. You can learn more about Jake at www.justjake.com.